THE MISSING

by

Stephen Zimmerman

This book is a work of fiction. Names, characters, places, and incidents are the product of the authors' imagination or are used fictitiously. Any resemblance to actual events, locales, or persons, living or dead, is coincidental.

Global Publishing Group LLC

Printed in the United States of America
Worldwide Distribution

First trade edition

ISBN 978-1-954804-16-6

CHAPTER ONE
HAMLIN

Detective Sam Cross hated small towns. All his life he'd lived in the Oklahoma City Metro. As strange as it sounds, he liked the traffic and lights and the bustle that comes with a major metropolitan area. Rural America just wasn't for him. Case in point: he'd arrived a few minutes earlier in Hamlin and still hadn't seen anyone, even though it was almost noon. He'd passed no cars on the road, seen no townsfolk walking the streets. No shopkeepers had been out sweeping their porches. A moment ago he'd parked across the street from the sheriff's office and walked over – only to be greeted by a sign on the door that said, "Sorry. Be back soon." Cross stood there on the steps, wiped a bead of sweat from his forehead, and looked around.

"The sheriff here probably thinks this is Mayberry and is out fishing," Cross muttered to himself. He pulled out his cell to call the number on the door and then rolled his eyes. "Of course, there's no cell service here," he said intentionally loud enough for anyone that might have been nearby to hear. As he walked back to his patrol car, the sun's reflection from a nearby shop door flashed in his eyes. Cross turned to look in the direction of the flash, but as he did the door quickly closed. *Odd*, he thought. *I thought small towns were known for their charm and friendliness. I guess Hamlin missed the memo.*

Prior to arriving, Cross had taken a second to look Hamlin up on Wikipedia. It was truly an uninteresting place – its only claim to fame being that it was named for a former Vice President. His GPS had also sent him on an unintended tour of the town. For some reason it had lost its mind as he entered the city limits. After several wrong directions, Cross had finally shut it off.

During his search for the sheriff's office, he'd seen a couple restaurants, including a Big-B Burger which would probably be where he'd end up for lunch in a few minutes. He'd also passed a dollar store, a grocery store, and a couple museums. The only other place that stood out to him was a city dump on the southeast side of town. After seeing way more of the town than he'd intended or cared to, he'd finally found the sheriff's office. And, of course, now it was closed.

He opened the door of his cruiser and leaned inside to get his radio when he got that uncanny feeling that someone was behind him. He turned around quickly to see the town sheriff standing there with a smile on his face that made Cross feel uneasy. A toothpick stuck out of his mouth.

"Long way from OKC aren't you, uh, Officer Cross," said the sheriff, peering at his name tag.

"It's Detective Cross, actually," Sam replied. "I got promoted last week but my new name tag was spelled wrong. I'm really not sure how you spell 'Cross' incorrectly, but someone managed it." Cross shifted under the sheriff's uncomfortable gaze. "I guess you're the sheriff here? What's your name? I don't see your name tag. Did they spell your name wrong too?" Cross chuckled but his joke flopped and didn't even produce a smile from the sheriff.

"Well, we're not too big on formalities around here. Seeing how I've been the sheriff for the last eighteen years, everyone just knows me as Sheriff Gunn or Gunny. Small town and all."

Then with a sudden sternness to his tone, Sheriff Gunn added, "You were just about to tell me what brings you to Hamlin."

"Of course," said Cross. "But I'd rather not discuss it here on the street. Can we go back to your office? Maybe get a cup of coffee?"

Sheriff Gunn grunted and nodded, and without further reply headed across the street toward the station. Cross called after him, "I was just about to try and radio back to my unit that I made it here. My cell phone doesn't have a signal." Sheriff Gunn either didn't hear him or, more likely, ignored him.

Wonderful, thought Cross sarcastically. *This assignment just keeps getting better and better*. He fiddled with his radio, but all he got was static, and so he locked the door to his car and headed for the station. Sheriff Gunn had already gone inside. Cross hoped the conversation would be quick – that he'd get the information he needed and be on his way.

Looking down the hall, Cross saw only one room with the door open and a light on, so he headed toward it figuring it must be the sheriff's office. It wasn't. It was instead some kind of file or records room. Maybe the evidence storage from past cases. It was surprisingly full of boxes, though Cross couldn't imagine that they had much crime to investigate in a small town like this.

"You just keep ending up in places you ain't supposed to be," said Sheriff Gunn behind him. That was twice the sheriff had sneaked up on him. For a big man, Sheriff Gunn managed to move rather quietly. "Office is this way," the sheriff said, flicking the light switch off as he closed and locked the door. "And sorry to disappoint you; there's no coffee."

"I just…" Cross began to say, but decided to let it go. They went around the corner, and there just past the restroom, Sheriff Gunn pointed to the room on the left. Cross had been in the car for the last several hours, and so he asked if he could use the restroom first. The sheriff nodded curtly. And then to Cross's further annoyance, as he stepped inside the small restroom, the sheriff stood outside the door like some kind of hall monitor.

As Cross washed up, he shook his head, frustrated at his misfortune to be given this case for his first assignment as a detective. He was pretty sure it was because he was the most junior detective in the office, and so he'd been given not only a boring assignment, but one that surely wouldn't do anything to pad his resume or advance his career.

Cross opened the bathroom door, and yep, still standing there was Sheriff Gunn. The whole situation had him so off kilter, he almost apologized for taking so long in the restroom. Cross was immediately thankful he hadn't.

Sheriff Gunn again pointed to the office without so much as a word. Cross entered the office and looked around. The sheriff walked behind his desk and sat in what looked like a very comfortable office chair. The only other seat in the office was a metal folding chair up against the wall. Cross opted to just stand, but Sheriff Gunn pointed at the chair and said, “Have a seat.” The metal chair was too small for his frame and Detective Cross was certain he looked silly sitting in it. In fact, Cross was sure that this was intentional. But whatever; this meeting would hopefully be short.

Once again Sheriff Gunn said curtly, “So, you were about to tell me why you’re here.”

“Yeah, uh, Sheriff, can I borrow your phone first for a minute? My cell doesn’t have service here, and I couldn’t get my radio to work either. I’d like to call back home and let my unit know that I made it, and maybe also call my wife and let her know I might be late for dinner.”

The sheriff replied, “Just call me Gunny, and we can see about a phone call after you tell me why you’re here.”

Well, that’s just stupid, thought Cross. *I’m a fellow cop, and I’m here on official police business, and yet I feel like I’m a suspect being interrogated.*

Sheriff Gunn, or Gunny as he’d told Cross to call him, raised his eyebrows and stared at him, so Cross dove into his explanation of what had brought him to Hamlin.

“Earlier this week, we got a report of a rather expensive sports car that was stolen from one of the ritzy neighborhoods in Oklahoma City. It had built-in GPS tracking. I was given the case and told to follow the GPS signal to see if I could recover it. The signal led me here to Hamlin but then my GPS went whacky – looked, though, like maybe it was pointing to the junkyard over on the southeast side of town. Instead of going straight there, I figured I'd come by your office and ask if you had seen anything. I'm just guessing that y'all probably don't have any quarter-of-a-million-dollar cars that belong here in Hamlin." Cross paused, took a breath and then continued.

"But then I kind of got lost, on account of my GPS, and so it took me a while to find your office. I did see that burger place, Big-B Burger. I was thinking about going there for lunch. Is it any good? Maybe we can grab a burger after this."

Cross didn't want to have lunch with the sheriff one bit and he was pretty sure the feeling was mutual, but he said it anyway to try to break the ice. Gunny continued to stare at Sam without answering.

"Oh," Cross added, "The car's a Ferrari 458 – red of course. I've got a picture from the owner here on my phone if you'd like to see, or I can give you a full-sheet printout from the case file out in my car."

Cross began to extend his phone toward the sheriff, but Gunny just waved it away and said, "Nope, we ain't had anything like that 'round here. We don't have much in the way of crime. The occasional domestic fight or property dispute, but nothing like car stealing. Though a couple decades back someone stole Granny Franklin's milk cow. But like I said, we're a quiet town. We keep to ourselves. We don't have much crime. We hardly get visitors..." and after a brief pause, Gunny added, "And we like it that way."

Well this seemed like a massive waste of time. Clearly the sheriff had no intention of helping him out – wouldn't even look at the picture and yet he was "so sure" that it wasn't here, despite the GPS signal indicating otherwise. Heck, Gunny probably drove a big pickup with a cattle guard on the front and had no clue what a Ferrari 458 looked like. Since he was getting nowhere with the sheriff, Cross began to stand up and take his leave.

"Going somewhere?" asked Gunny.

"Well, like I said, I think I'll get a burger, and then if it's all the same to you, I'll be getting on with my investigation. I didn't drive two hours out here to your lovely city to go home without looking around for that car. Like I said, the GPS tracker showed very clearly that the stolen car should be here in Hamlin somewhere. Again, looked like maybe over by the dump, so I figured I'll look there first. This being my first case and all as a detective, I'd like to make a good impression on my supervisor and wrap things up today if possible."

With the mention of Cross investigating the dump, Sheriff Gunn's eyes got wide, and he shifted uncomfortably in his chair. Gunny had tried to hide this reaction, but Cross noticed. So, Cross figured he'd mention it again.

"Isn't the dump over on Jeffery Street? I'll just swing by there after I grab a burger."

Yep, same reaction from the sheriff when Cross mentioned the dump again. There was clearly something about it that made the sheriff nervous. Surely the sheriff wasn't involved with the theft of the Ferrari. Gunny was gruff and borderline rude, but Cross didn't necessarily get the vibe from the sheriff that he was a dirty cop.

Gunny never answered him, so Cross said a courteous "Thanks," and headed for the door. Gunny sat back in his chair with his mind clearly on something else. Cross figured he'd head outside again and see if he could get a cell signal. Maybe Big-B Burger had Wi-Fi. Who was he kidding though – not likely in a small town like this.

As Cross exited out onto the steps, he got the distinct feeling that he was being watched, even though he didn't see anybody. Suddenly the sheriff burst out of the door behind him, almost hitting him with the door. Cross jumped back, nearly lost his footing, barely catching himself from falling down the steps.

That would've been embarrassing, Cross thought. "What gives?" he said out loud to the sheriff.

"Uh, excuse me. I've got an errand to run," said Gunny as he hurried toward the rear parking lot behind the station.

Cross replied, "Well, I'm going to see if I can get a signal on my cell or figure out my radio malfunction, so I can get a call in back home. See you later."

Gunny stopped, his back to Cross. He looked for a second like he was going to turn around, but then he took a few more steps. Finally Gunny spun around and said, "Son, we need to have a talk – but not here. Back inside."

If it was possible for Cross to be more annoyed than he already was, it further irritated him that Gunny called him "son." The sheriff didn't look *that* much older than he was; certainly not more than five or ten years.

Back to the sheriff's office they both went. Gunny sat down on the edge of the desk and once again pointed to the metal folding chair. Cross just stood this time. Gunny cleared his throat and then began to speak.

"About your phone and radio, you're not going to find a signal. Our town is…different. Electronic devices not on our network don't work here. And you're not going to be able to call out on my phone either. We don't have long distance calling here in Hamlin; just local calls is all."

Cross's mind was blown. *What is this? The stone age?* he thought with bewilderment. He'd never heard of such a thing. And it's one thing to not be able to get a cell signal, but to be told that his phone wouldn't work *at all* here in Hamlin – and his radio too? And no long distance? This was preposterous. The whole thing was ridiculous. This was supposed to be an easy "newbie" case.

And he had to contact his police unit and his wife. Maybe he'd just leave and tell his supervisor that the local sheriff was uncooperative and see what he wanted him to do.

No, he could just hear his boss' voice, "Junior Detective Sam Cross..." (his boss had been making a point all week to call him 'junior detective') "...you can't handle a grumpy small-town sheriff? How are you ever going to be a real crime fighter? Don't make me assign another detective to this case!"

No, if Cross knew what was good for him, he'd stay here, make the best of things, and solve this case on his own – or he'd never hear the end of it back at the squad room.

Gunny continued, "And there ain't no reason to be poking around at the dump. Ain't nothing over there to see. Junk is all. I'm sure this missing Ferrari of yours isn't there – or anywhere here in Hamlin."

Gunny's voice had lost its former gruffness. In fact, Cross was almost sure the sheriff sounded scared. But of what Cross didn't know. Maybe there was more to this city than what meets the eye.

Cross replied, "Well I think I'm just going to go ahead and head out then after a bit. Maybe drive back up the road a ways and see if I get a signal on the highway. And perhaps book a hotel up near I-40 in case I don't wrap things up tonight." He really needed to contact the station back home and his wife.

"We've got hotels here," said Gunny, almost pleadingly.

"Just the same," answered Cross, "I'm going to eat lunch, do my job, and then head out before dark."

At this, Gunny practically yelled at him, "You can't leave!"

"What?" exclaimed Cross.

"It's not just you," said the sheriff, his voice returning to a normal volume, though it still sounded strained. "It's everyone, town folk included. No one's supposed to come in; my head's gonna roll as it is from you being here. But no one leaves Hamlin." The sheriff, after a pause, said in a low voice, "And I'm afraid, Detective Cross, that now means you too."

CHAPTER TWO
TIFFANY

Detective Cross stood there stunned. His mind raced in a million directions. Was Sheriff Gunn for real? Was he a hostage? Should he be reaching for his gun? Should he make a run for it? What was going on with this town?

Time seemed to stand still, though probably only a couple seconds passed. Blood pounded in his ears as his adrenaline surged. Cross wasn't buff, but he was in good shape. He quickly sized up Gunny in case he had to fight his way out. Unfortunately, Gunny was bigger and looked like he'd been through a scrape or two and would probably whoop him in a fight.

Gunny must've noticed Cross's reaction to the news that he couldn't leave because the sheriff quickly added, "I ain't got nothing against you, Detective. We're on the same side. But that's just the way it is here in Hamlin. Our city was chosen, I suppose, because of its out-of-the-way location. We ain't got no choice. Been this way for half a century now, I guess. I'll take you over and get you a room at the hotel and help you get settled in, now that you're here."

"Wait, what? I have zero intentions of staying here!" exclaimed Cross. How could the sheriff be so calm about everything? Get him a room and help him settle in?

Gunny ignored his outburst. "Big-B Burger is pretty good, probably the best burger joint in town. You'll like it. Mrs. Franklin – that's the daughter of Granny Franklin, God rest her soul – serves the best sweet tea there too. And they also got pretty good fries, though the fries over at Rival's Sports Bar and Grill might be just a touch better."

What is going on? Cross was starting to wonder if the sheriff might have lost his grip on reality. Had small town living been so boring that his brain concocted a horrific tale just to add excitement? Cross supposed it was possible. At this point, anything was possible.

"You're welcome to drive around and see the sights of Hamlin as much as you like, but I warn you..." Gunny said, his voice regaining its gruffness, "...put out of your mind whatever thoughts you have of leaving. They'll stop you for sure, and they just might take you away with them. Wouldn't want you to go missing."

This can't be happening, thought Cross. There was no way any of this was real. Was this the kind of jokes they thought were funny in small towns like Hamlin? None of this made sense. Every word the sheriff spoke raised more questions in his mind. What did he mean their city was "chosen?" And who were "they" that were going to try and stop him from leaving?

Cross finally found his voice and stammered, "I'm sure you think this is all very funny. But seriously, I've got a job to do and I intend to be out of here before sunset."

Gunny looked him square in the eye and said, "I ain't kidding, son. Get you your burger. Talk to Mr.

Olsen over at the Freeway Inn, or if you like there's a nice bed and breakfast downtown called Gena's. But don't leave town. It just ain't possible." He took a breath and continued. "Now it's almost one o'clock and like I told you earlier, I've got an errand to run. If you know what's good for you, you'll mind what I said. But I'm serious as a heart attack about not leaving. Oh, and you'd best forget about your investigation and that missing car. Folks don't take too kindly to strangers, or anyone for that matter, poking their nose where it don't belong."

Cross started to speak, but the sheriff held up his hand and cut him off. He simply pointed to the door and motioned with his hat for Cross to leave. Once outside, the sheriff locked the office door, put his hat on his head, and once again headed around the back of the station, presumably toward his car. Cross was left standing stunned on the steps. Just before the sheriff turned the corner, he called over his shoulder, "Remember, son, what I said!" And just like that he was gone.

Cross heard a diesel engine start up, and from behind the building came Sheriff Gunn in a big pickup truck complete with a cattle guard on the front. At least Cross had gotten something right. Cross walked quickly to the passenger side of the pickup. Gunny rolled the window down halfway. "If it's not you, who exactly is it then that won't let me leave?" Cross asked.

"Hive. Nasty lot. Don't cross them – no pun intended."

Before Sam could say anything else, Gunny rolled the window back up and off he went with a rumble. He watched until Gunny turned south and then disappeared out of sight.

Cross stood there experiencing a mixture of anger and confusion. He had a ton of questions, but it seemed that Sheriff Gun wouldn't be any help. So if the sheriff wouldn't answer them, he'd find someone who would. He remembered seeing the door to a nearby store open slightly and then close so he headed that way. It was the hardware store, but when he pulled on the handle, it was surprisingly locked. He peered inside. All the lights were on, but there was no sign of anyone. Another thing to add to the list of odd occurrences in this town.

Cross was no longer hungry. The meeting with the sheriff had ruined his appetite, but he knew if he skipped lunch he'd probably get a migraine, so he made up his mind to head over and get something at Big-B Burger – and maybe get some answers from Mrs. Franklin, too. As he walked back to his cruiser, he looked up to the sky as if to say to heaven, *Why me, Lord?*

He got into his car. After the way his day was going so far, Cross half expected his car not to start or something. It, of course, started and as he backed out of his parking spot, he caught sight of the door to the hardware store, crack open again. "Unbelievable," grumbled Cross.

What should have been a short drive to Big-B Burger ended up taking longer due to two wrong turns thanks to his inoperable GPS. He thought about digging his atlas out of the trunk, but then decided that Hamlin was far too small to be detailed on the map. Finally, he arrived at Big-B's. As he surveyed the parking lot, only one other car was there. He walked through the door which gave a loud ding. From the back came a young, college-age girl. This obviously wasn't Mrs. Franklin. She was much too young to be the daughter of "Granny Franklin" like Gunny had described. The young lady froze in the doorway and her eyes got big when she saw him. After a moment, she forced a strained smile and walked to the counter, saying nothing.

Cross broke the awkward silence by ordering the mushroom Swiss burger special. The cashier finally spoke by asking what drink he'd like with his meal. Cross answered, "The sweet tea." As Cross paid, he thanked her by name, reading it off her name tag. "Thank you, Tiffany."

Tiffany blushed and stammered, "How'd you know my name?" But before Cross could answer, she nervously laughed and said, "Oh yeah, my nametag." She then headed to the back without another word.

Cross had the place to himself, so he chose the booth in the corner where his back would be against a wall, but he'd still have a view of the entire restaurant and the street outside. This position also afforded him the ability to hear what was going on in the back of the restaurant.

He heard Tiffany say loudly, "Mrs. Franklin, there's a stranger in the lobby."

"A stranger!" exclaimed Mrs. Franklin in a loud whisper. "Keep your voice down. Who is it?"

"I don't know, ma'am," said Tiffany more subdued, "but he's got a police uniform on. His nametag says Cross."

"A police officer," repeated Mrs. Franklin. "I wonder if Gunny knows he's here. Good Lord, I'd better call him. You'd best get over there and make his food."

Cross resisted the urge to shout through the door that he'd already met Gunny, but as much as the idea amused him, he kept quiet. He pulled out his phone again. Still no service. To his surprise, there was Wi-Fi. He quickly tried to connect, but it popped up asking for a password. Rats.

After about ten minutes, he saw the door to the back of the restaurant begin to open, but before anyone came through, he again heard the loud whisper of Mrs. Franklin say, "Tiffany, be friendly to the man. See what you can learn, but don't make him suspicious."

The door opened the rest of the way and Tiffany walked out of the back and looked around, clearly not expecting Cross to be sitting in the corner. He gave a small wave and put on a fake smile as she headed his way.

"Here's your mushroom Swiss burger, fries, and sweet tea. Can I get you anything else, sir?"

"No," Cross said. "Mustard's right here on the table, so I guess that's it."

She hesitated next to the table as Cross bit into the burger. Finally, she asked, "Officer Cross, is it? Do you mind if I pull up a chair and sit for a minute? My work's done in the back and we're kind of slow right now. Besides that, we don't get many out-of-towners."

Cross had hoped to talk to Mrs. Franklin, but this Tiffany girl seemed perhaps an easier mark to get answers from. "Sure," said Cross. "And by the way, it's Detective Cross. They misspelled my name on my new nametag, so I had to keep wearing my old one." Why did he keep telling people that?

"But you can just call me Sam. Things don't seem very formal here in Hamlin."

"My name's Tiffany Gunn, but you can just call me Tiff or Tiffany, if you like."

Gunn. So she was related somehow to the sheriff. Daughter maybe? He'd find out.

"So I briefly met the sheriff earlier," Sam said. It wasn't entirely truthful, but he didn't want to let on how much he'd already been told. "Saw his last name was Gunn too. Any relation?"

Tiffany's eyes widened, and she said, "Yea – I mean, yes Sir. He's my dad."

"That's okay," Sam said, "You don't have to call me 'Sir.' Sam is fine, or Detective Cross if you prefer."

"Okay, Sam," Tiffany replied. "Where are you from? What brings you to town?"

"I'm from Oklahoma City. Came out this way for a case I'm working on. But I'm just passing through and decided to stop to get a burger for a late lunch." Again, not the whole truth, but since she'd been sent by Mrs. Franklin to get information from him, he would control what and how much she got.

"I might stay the night though," Sam continued. "Would you recommend The Freeway Inn or Gena's?"

"Gena's," Tiffany said quickly and almost sharply. She corrected her tone however and added, "It's closer and Mrs. Gena's real nice. She always makes blueberry pancakes for breakfast."

"Well, I'll make up my mind after a while. Might just go ahead and leave town though." Sam looked to see if she'd react to the prospect of him leaving town. She did. She'd been looking down, kind of shyly, but he noticed her back stiffen and her head snap up when he mentioned leaving town.

"I'd probably – I'd definitely stay the night if I were you," Tiffany urged. "It's nearly two already, and it's a long drive back to Oklahoma City." Her voice held the same pleading tone her dad's voice had conveyed back at the station.

Sam got the message loud and clear. Though she didn't say it as directly as her father had, Sam understood he was being cautioned not to leave town. *Hmm. So, the sheriff wasn't kidding after all*, thought Sam. He was worried by what this meant, but the cop in him also made him all the more suspicious.

Tiffany had gotten up to refill his tea, so when she returned Sam asked her about the missing car. "So I've been tracking a stolen sports car. Red, very expensive. Have you seen or heard anything?"

"Nope. Nothing. We're just a quiet little town," Tiffany said evasively.

Interesting, thought Sam. She hadn't seemed particularly surprised he was looking for an expensive car, but she had been quick to dismiss the inquiry.

"So what's there to do around town?" Sam asked. "I saw a city dump on the southeast side. Anything fun to do there?" Sam probed.

At that Tiffany's eyes got really wide, and she suddenly stood up and said, "I'd better get back to work." She rushed away in such a hurry that she left her wash rag balled up on the table.

Sam finished up the rest of his meal and sipped the sweet tea deep in thought. The sheriff had been right. It was good sweet tea; sweet but not too syrupy. On a napkin, Sam wrote out what he knew so far.

About fifty years ago someone, or some kind of criminal enterprise perhaps, had taken over the town, and now the townsfolk were held in fear. No one was allowed to leave and no one was supposed to get in. It was unclear to Sam how he'd bypassed whatever security was supposed to be in place. That made Sam think: maybe if it had been so easy to get in, it would be equally easy to get out. It was worth a shot.

There was also something mysterious about the city dump. A mere mention of the word seemed to make folks nervous – first the sheriff and now his daughter. Sam determined to see what that was all about, despite the sheriff's warning. Also, for some reason, his phone and his radio didn't work here. On his way over to Big-B's, he'd looked for a pay phone without success. No real surprise though; this was the twenty-first century – even if Hamlin seemed stuck a few decades behind.

Sam's thoughts were interrupted. From the back of the restaurant came a short, heavyset woman with red hair. She looked to be about fifty-five.

"Howdy, ma'am," Sam said. "Where's Tiffany? I'd like some more of this delicious sweet tea."

The woman replied, "I'm Mrs. Franklin, the owner. Tiffany's shift ended early, and she's gone home for the day. I'll get you your tea."

As Mrs. Franklin approached the table with his refill she asked, "What brings you to Hamlin, Officer?"

"It's detective, ma'am, and I'm just passing through on police business out of Oklahoma City. To be honest, I best be going." Sam wasn't sure if she was a friend or foe, and so he decided it was best not to engage further in conversation, especially considering he'd already talked at length to Tiffany. He was disappointed Tiffany had left so suddenly. He had been hoping to use her for more information. He dropped a five dollar bill on the table as a tip, and with Mrs. Franklin watching him like a hawk he headed to his squad car.

To Sam's surprise, on the parking barrier in front of his car sat Tiffany. She was hunched over close to the bumper of the car as if trying to stay out of sight of the restaurant. Sam glanced back over his shoulder. Mrs. Franklin was still watching him through the window, though she retreated to the back of the restaurant when he looked in her direction.

Sam began to walk to the front of the car where Tiffany was sitting, but she held a finger to her lips and motioned him to stop. Sam instead walked normally to the door of his cruiser as though he hadn't seen her, and without looking at her spoke in a somewhat hushed voice,"Is there something I can do for you Tiffany? Mrs. Franklin said you'd gone home."

Tiffany replied, her voice barely above a whisper, "Yes Sir, I mean Sam. I need to talk to you. But I can't have anyone see us together. Can I ride with you? We could drive over to this quiet spot by the lake where no one will be watching."

Sam hesitated. As a married man, he considered that it might be a bad idea letting an attractive, blonde, college-age girl fifteen years his junior into his car – especially considering that she'd just suggested they drive to a secluded spot. There was no way he'd say yes to that back in Oklahoma City, but considering all the strange occurrences of the day and how scared she seemed to be at the moment, he nodded and pushed the button to unlock the passenger door. With a low crouch, Tiffany hurried to the passenger side of the car, opened the door just enough to slip inside, and ducked in, sliding down in her seat below the level of the window.

"Where to?" Sam asked. "You'll have to give me directions. My GPS isn't working."

Tiffany paused to get her bearings and then said, "Um, turn right out of here and drive north five blocks. When you get to Lily Street, turn left and drive about a mile and you'll see the lake. There's a pavilion there to the right where we can talk. No one ever comes to the lake anymore so we should be safe."

Sam drove in silence. Tiffany stayed hunched down in the seat nervously biting a fingernail. After about five minutes, Sam saw the lake just as Tiffany had said. He looked right, and sure enough, there was the pavilion. The park looked deserted, so Sam parked the car out of sight of the road as best as he could and informed Tiffany that they had arrived.

"No black SUVs followed you did they?" Tiffany asked.

Sam wished she'd mentioned that earlier. Driving in an unfamiliar town, he'd mostly paid attention to the street signs and turns. He hadn't really been looking to see if anyone was following him, though he figured he'd notice something as obvious as a black SUV, and so he said no. Tiffany breathed a sigh of relief, and Sam did too, not even realizing he'd been somewhat holding his breath.

They walked over to the pavilion, and before he could ask her what was going on, she blurted out, "You can't leave town, they'll take you away or kill you or worse – I don't know, but you can't leave!" And having said that, she burst into tears.

Sam stood there in silence not knowing what to say. Tiffany walked over and sat on a picnic table under the pavilion and put her face in her hands. A few moments later, Tiffany wiped her tears away with the back of her hand and apologized.

"No apology necessary." Sam smiled, trying to make her feel better. "Just tell me what's going on. Why can't I leave?"

This set her off crying again, but through her tears she said, "It's the rule. No one can ever leave Hamlin. And anyone who tries or doesn't do exactly what they're told goes missing."

Sheriff Gunn had said something about "going missing" back at the office, but Cross had dismissed it as an idle threat. But now Tiffany had said it again.

"Missing?" Sam questioned. "Who takes them? Where do people go?"

Tiffany stood up and paced a few steps. "We're not supposed to talk about it." Her voice then took on a bitter tone and her cheeks flushed bright red with anger. "But I'm tired of being quiet. I'm tired of pretending everything in our stupid town is normal. I'm tired of people I love going missing."

She took a deep, ragged breath and continued, "I don't really know much about who takes them." She blinked back more tears. "We're not supposed to ask questions. They call themselves The Hive. They've been in control of the town forever. My dad says they arrived a dozen or so years before he was born. He's forty-two last year, almost forty-three. He acts like he's not afraid of them, but I know he is. They make him guard the main road into town to keep strangers from coming in. I don't know how you made it in past him."

"He wasn't there," replied Sam. "I just drove into town about eleven this morning and didn't see anyone until I talked to your dad when I stopped at the sheriff's office."

"Oh," Tiffany said, biting her lip worriedly. "I hope he doesn't get in trouble. Supposedly the previous sheriff screwed up and he went missing too. That's when dad took over." At the thought of this, she sobbed again.

Sam wasn't sure what to make of her story. Maybe it was all true. Maybe none of it was true – just a ghost story to scare the townsfolk into submission. Sam changed the subject from her father to distract her. "Do you know where the Hive came from?"

"No," Tiffany said as she sniffled. "Dad never talks about them much – ever really. I guess they just appeared one day and moved in. There were only about 5,000 residents back then and they just took over. Supposedly folks tried to telephone out for help, but the phones wouldn't work for some reason."

"Yeah I know the feeling," Sam said holding up his cell phone. "Can't get a signal ever since I came into town. The radio in my cruiser won't work either. You don't have a working cell phone by any chance do you?"

Tiffany nodded. "I do, but it won't do you any good. Something makes it where you can only call numbers on a predetermined list. Just local numbers here in town. And they monitor every call you make too, so even if you could somehow call out of town, they'd know about it. Land lines are the same way."

Sam narrowed his eyes and furrowed his brow. This all seemed impossible. Just then an idea came to him. "What about the internet? I saw there was Wi-Fi at Big-B's earlier, but I couldn't get on without a password."

Tiffany shrugged. "I can't get on it either. Mrs. Franklin won't give me the password. We've got internet at home, but Hive controls what websites you can get on. If you try to go to an unapproved site, it gets blocked, and you get a message saying that the Hive is monitoring your traffic. So I just go to cooking websites and stuff like that. Maybe one day I'll have my own restaurant like Mrs. Franklin."

Tiffany eventually ran out of things to say, so they sat there in silence. Sam struggled to make sense in his mind of the events of the day and what Tiffany had now told him. Every question he asked seemed to bring up three new ones. Who was Hive? Where did they come from? How many were in their organization? What made them so powerful that an entire town, including its armed sheriff, would be afraid of them? And what did they want with Hamlin?

The silence became awkward, so Sam stood up and motioned toward the car. "Come on, I'll drop you off, and then I'm going to drive around town a bit. I'm going to see if I can get to the bottom of this Hive business. I came here to investigate and I plan to do just that."

Tiffany seemed suddenly inspired by this and declared, "I wanna come with you."

"No, no, no," Sam said. "It'll likely be dangerous. I'm a trained cop and detective. I'll be better alone."

"You need me," Tiffany insisted. "And I need you."

Sam shook his head no, but Tiffany was persistent. "I know my way around town. I know where the safe spots are. I know who can be trusted and who can't. Plus, I want to find my friend Laura. She went missing last week. She tried to leave to go to college in OKC, but they stopped her. When she tried to run, they took her away. She's been missing ever since."

Sam pursed his lips. *I don't really need a girl tagging along,* he thought. It was one more back to watch besides his own – but she had a point. He didn't know his way around town. If she hadn't mentioned the black SUVs he wouldn't have known to watch for them. She'd told him so much already that he had no reason not to trust her. Plus, she'd be able to recognize Laura if he came across her.

She stared at him with her hands on her hips waiting for his answer.

Sam sighed. "Fine. You can for now, but if things get crazy, I don't want to put you in danger. And you got to listen to me, okay?"

With his answer, she suddenly hugged him and then ran to the car. Sam was taken back, but she called, "Come on Sam, let's get going!"

Sam walked to the car. "I think it's best for today if I still drop you off. The afternoon's about gone, and I don't want your dad or anyone else suspicious of you not being home. Plus, I need to get over to Gena's and get a room. Can I meet you here tomorrow? How far away do you live?"

"That's fine I suppose," Tiffany said disappointed. "You know what, I don't live but about half a mile. I'll just walk from here. I'm off work tomorrow, so I can meet you any time."

"Alright," Sam said, "Sounds good. Let's plan on an early start of 9:00AM." Although now as he thought more about it, Sam considered missing their meeting. Perhaps he'd try to sneak out of town under cover of darkness. So he added, "And if I don't show up for whatever reason, don't wait around for me. I might get delayed by something."

"I'll be here," Tiffany said with a smile and then waved goodbye. She turned and headed east, presumably toward her house. Sam stayed there another couple minutes to collect his thoughts and then drove back into town to find Gena's. He wished he'd asked Tiffany for directions, but hey, it's a small town; he'd find it eventually – and maybe stumble across something useful.

As he entered the main part of town, he noticed a black SUV parked under the awning of the Elementary School. He'd driven past the school on his way to the lake and now he hoped that the SUV hadn't been there before. But he had no way of knowing. He tried to look inside the windows as he drove by, but it was either empty or the tinted windows and shadows kept him from seeing anyone.

He eventually came upon a large, historic, two-story house painted white and sky blue. A small green sign with black lettering out front said "Gena's." Sam pulled next to the curb, locked the car doors, and walked up the sidewalk toward the front door. That uneasy feeling of being watched by several pairs of eyes returned. Not wanting to look suspicious, Sam resisted the urge to look around and instead just reached for the door handle.

CHAPTER THREE
HIVE

Tiffany arrived home and called out a “Hello” as she came through the door. There was no answer. She squinted at the grandfather clock in the entryway. It read a little after 4:00PM. She kicked off her shoes and then walked into the kitchen. The light was off, and there was no sign of her dad. She peaked out the backdoor window; no sign of him out back either.

The sheriff’s office closed at 4:00PM, but maybe Dad had stopped at a store on the way home. Tiffany went to her room, peeled off her jeans and Big-B Burger shirt, and slipped on a pair of comfy grey shorts and a green crop top. Summers in Oklahoma could be brutally hot and humid, and today was such a day. *Glad to be out of those clothes,* she thought. She grabbed a can of pop and plopped down on the couch. She switched on an old sitcom rerun just because that’s what she always did after work, but her mind was elsewhere.

What a wild day, she thought. What started off as just another mundane day in their little town had all been changed by the arrival of Sam Cross, the detective out of Oklahoma City. Hamlin rarely had visitors. It was one of her dad’s jobs as sheriff to discourage passersby from entering their town. If a traveler couldn’t be talked into taking an alternate route, so long as they only passed through or stopped for a bite to eat, some gas, or an overnight stay at the hotel, and moved on without causing any trouble, *usually* nothing more came of it. But that was all up to the discretion of Hive. She could think of twice where a stranger was forbidden to leave – though there might've been more. One of the strangers, a widow lady, had been "persuaded" to stay. She now ran Gena's, the bed and breakfast downtown. The other stranger, a cattle rancher, supposedly put up a big fight and made a run for it, and that was the last anyone had seen of him. Probably meant he joined the Missing, as the townsfolk called them. Tiffany wasn't sure why Hive didn't allow these two to leave. Maybe it was random. Maybe they had another unknown reason.

Hive usually kept a low profile – but just enough presence to keep a feeling of fear over the town. In fact, Tiffany had only seen a member of Hive up close a couple dozen or so times in her life, and each time had weirded her out. But since they were usually unseen, she rarely thought about them, especially since few people around town would talk about them. But ever since her best friend Laura went missing last week, Tiffany had spent most of her free time trying to figure out what she could. The Hive members always wore black. Sometimes they wore what looked like a paramilitary uniform, complete with a black beret, and sometimes they wore black suits. She'd never really seen one of their faces fully because the ones in the paramilitary uniforms wore black masks, and the ones in suits always wore dark sunglasses – plus she really hadn't tried to look because she didn't want to be caught staring.

Last Sunday she'd met her dad at his office for lunch, and while he was over at Rival's Sports Bar and Grill getting some wings for them to share, she'd been able to take a look for a few minutes in the records room at the station. One thing she'd discovered is that the population of the town had been steadily declining for the past fifty-five years. At the town's height in 1960, the population had been almost 5,200. Certainly not a booming city by any means, but still a fair bit more than the present day. The 2010 census showed just 3,765. She'd done some quick math later at home, and accounting for those who died of natural causes, roughly twenty people per year mysteriously disappeared. She wasn't sure how many total Missing there were, but she estimated somewhere between 1,000 and 1,500. And when she counted out those she knew personally who were now missing, she could think of nearly fifty. Tiffany sighed loudly as she thought over the magnitude of the toll Hive had taken on their town. Fifty people she'd known during her life that now no one knew where they'd gone. She knew people went missing every year, but she'd never thought about just how many – that is until Laura went missing too.

She'd felt angry and cried a lot this week, of course being careful not to let her dad, Mrs. Franklin, or anyone else see her. The last thing Tiffany wanted was to have to explain herself, especially since everyone was supposed to pretend that everything was normal all the time and smile and say cheerful "Howdy's" to those they passed on the street.

Based upon the census data she'd uncovered, as best as Tiffany could tell, Hive had taken over their town around 1960, and had been in control of Hamlin ever since. She'd never really thought about it until now, but since it was 2015, that meant that this year was the fifty-fifth "anniversary" of the Takeover. That was how it was referenced in a few of the files she'd seen at her dad's office, though she'd never personally heard anyone call it that. But not like anyone hardly ever talked about it anyway. She'd brought it up once or twice to her dad over the years, and he always gave a gruff, curt answer and changed the subject.

Another thing that bothered Tiffany was that her dad never talked about her mom. He'd even taken down all the family photos of them together and stored them in his bedroom closet. The last memory Tiffany had of her mom was her fifth birthday party. She'd had a unicorn cake and got her first skates, and Mom had helped her try them on. Best as Tiffany could remember, Mom was gone less than a week later. Dad had told her at the time that Mom had left them and moved away to Texas. Tiffany had tried over the years to get her dad to open up, but every time she asked, he'd clam up or retreat to his bedroom. Now, with all she'd learned this last week, Tiffany wondered if Mom was one of the Missing. They'd even had a big fight about it on Monday.

"I don't believe you!" Tiffany had accused. "I don't know if mom's dead, or run away with another man, or what – but why would she just go to Texas? And why didn't you go after her? Didn't you love her?"

"Of course I loved her – more than anything," her dad had answered. She could still remember the hurt in his eyes from her accusation.

"Dad, I miss her every day," Tiffany had pleaded. "I don't know why we can't at least have her pictures up. It's like you don't want to remember she even existed."

Her dad had said nothing else. He'd just grabbed a beer and headed to his bedroom as usual.

Tiffany hadn't been able to investigate any further because her search through the files at the sheriff's office had been cut short by the rumble of her dad's truck returning with their lunch. She'd hurriedly closed the file cabinet, shut off the light and dashed to the restroom by her dad's office to allow her heart to stop racing and her hands to stop shaking before joining her dad. It was Thursday now and as much as she wanted to take another peek in the files, things just hadn't worked out. And she had to be careful not to make her dad suspicious – or worse, get caught in that room.

The grandfather clock in the hallway began to chime and she looked up at the TV. A new episode of her show had started. The clock chimed five times meaning she'd been daydreaming for the last fifty minutes. She got up, adjusted her shorts that had ridden up uncomfortably, and looked out the front window. Odd. Dad's still hadn't come home. "What could possibly be keeping him?" she wondered out loud. Maybe he'd stopped to check in on Grandpa Bill. Her dad did that every so often, on account of Grandpa Bill's age. Sometimes he brought Grandpa Bill home for supper too.

She returned to her spot on the sofa, but couldn't concentrate on the TV show. She'd seen this episode half a dozen times anyway – shows in Hamlin were always reruns. She got up and checked the clock again. Quarter after five now.

Minutes turned into hours and Dad still hadn't come home. She'd called twice and sent him five or six texts, but he hadn't answered. It was dark now. She'd tried to snack, but worry stole her appetite. She fought back tears. What if her dad had gone missing now too? All she could do was pray to a God she wasn't even sure cared about their little town.

***

7 hours earlier

Sheriff Gunn shouted back to Detective Cross, warning him to listen to what he'd told him about not leaving town or poking around, and then he walked quickly to his pickup. He was beating himself up mentally for being so careless and letting the detective into town. He'd been over at the music store looking at a guitar he was thinking about getting Tiffany for her birthday next week. He wasn't supposed to leave his post until his shift ended at noon, but it was so boring sitting his shift on the main road with how rarely travelers came their way. They *were* pretty far off the beaten path. But in the thirty minutes – for sure not more than an hour that he'd been away from his post – Detective Cross had slipped in. Though since Cross had come on police business, it's doubtful he could've turned him back anyway.

Now Gunny had the unsavory job of reporting his mistake to his contact at Hive – though knowing Hive, they already knew. He'd have to think of a better story than "birthday shopping." It was a quick drive to the dump where the entrance to the Hive base was located, but, once inside, it usually took as much as twenty minutes to be seen. Even someone like him, the town sheriff, didn't have a fast track to speak with a Hive agent.

As he sat in his truck, some classic country playing quietly in the background, his cell phone rang. It startled him, and he whacked his elbow on the window grabbing for it. He muttered a swear word under his breath, rubbed his elbow and looked down at the phone. It was Mrs. Franklin. He answered and listened as she nervously told him that Cross had stopped in at Big-B's. He assured her that he'd already handled it and told her to act normal.

Gunny hung up his phone and looked up, nearly jumping out of his skin again. There, standing outside his pickup window was a Hive agent. They always gave him the willies anyway, and being startled by one made it worse. He rolled down his window and listened to the muffled instructions spoken by the masked Hive agent. A rusty metal gate disguised the Hive base to make it look like an ordinary city dump. With the push of a few numbers on a small keypad, it slid noiselessly open. The agent motioned with his rifle for Gunny to drive forward. Once through the gate it closed just as silently behind him. He drove around to the side of a prefab building that to the uninitiated person would look like only an office or large shed.

Gunny rang the buzzer and after several moments, a soft click indicated the lock had been opened. He opened the door and headed down the staircase that lay in front of him. The stairwell was lit by small red lights on the sides of each step. There was no handrail and so Gunny was careful as he descended. At the bottom was just one door. Once again he rang the small red-lit buzzer and waited. Thankfully this time, the door unlocked almost immediately. Inside was the large bunker-like room where he always met with his Hive contact: a tall, slender, self-important man he knew only as Agent Grant. Gunny hated when someone had a name like "Grant" or "Reed" that could be a first or a last name because he never knew which it was.

In the center of the room was a black metal desk. Behind it was an empty black chair where he expected Agent Grant to be seated. Agent Grant was nowhere to be seen. Gunny chose to wait for Agent Grant by the door since there were no other seats available.

As he waited, he looked around the room. On the far-left wall, running the entire length of it was a gun rack lined with black rifles like the one carried by the agent at the gate outside. On the wall in front of him were two large, identical flags bearing the Hive emblem.

The Hive flag reminded him somewhat of the Marine Corp flag: red in color with a similar emblem in the middle. But where the globe would be in the Marine Corp design, there was instead a hideous, almost alien-looking face – if you could call it that, with several smaller identical faces surrounding it. And instead of an eagle on top, there was what Gunny assumed was a queen bee or wasp. Barbed wire or perhaps thorns bordered the emblem on each side. Gunny wasn't sure which. He'd never looked that closely and he didn't care to ask.

The right wall was unadorned, except for a couple posters that were too far away for him to make out what they said. He was turning forty-three this year, but refused to break down and get glasses that he probably needed. In the middle of the wall was a door that led to who knows where. Gunny had never been beyond this room. But supposedly there is a vast network – practically a city which ran for miles underground where Hive did whatever it was they did. That's if you believed the whispered rumors from fearful townsfolk. Gunny didn't though. He'd never seen any excavating equipment or heard the sounds of construction that such an operation would surely elicit.

But who knows. And he knew better than to ask questions. He'd learned a long time ago to just keep his head down, mind his own business, and do what he's told. He hated that last part. He hated Hive with everything in him. He hated being their pawn. But he didn't want to become the next to join the Missing. And so for the last almost twenty years he'd been sheriff, he'd done exactly as he was told. He also had Tiffany to think of.

After what seemed like forever, without a sound, the door in the right wall opened and in walked Agent Grant. And there was someone with him. It was a short woman in a tight-fitting green uniform. The woman appeared to be athletic in build with shoulder length brown hair. He had never seen this female agent before.

"Please, Sheriff Gunn, come forward," said Agent Grant. The way he smiled and his unusual friendliness made Gunny uneasy. "Come on, come on, right up to the desk," urged Agent Grant entirely too cheerfully. The woman said nothing, and to Gunny's surprise, she, not Agent Grant, sat down in the black chair behind the desk. Agent Grant stood to her right.

"I have someone here who's very interested in meeting you. Meet Grand Matron Elektra Von Druska, leader of Hive."

The blood drained from Gunny's face. He knew of the Grand Matron, but he'd never actually met her before. His mind raced to all kinds of horrible reasons she wanted to see him, beginning with allowing Detective Cross into town.

The Grand Matron finally spoke with a cold voice that sent chills of dread to Gunny's bones. "We have a situation don't we, Paul?" she said with a slight accent that Gunny couldn't place. And though her voice made his skin crawl, there was something seductive about it as well.

A wave of nausea washed over him as she said his first name. No one but his mother and his wife had ever called him Paul. Why would she use his first name like that? It suddenly occurred to Gunny that the interruption of Mrs. Franklin's phone call had completely made him forget to think of a lie to explain why he had left his post. And now, with the Grand Matron before him, staring him down, Gunny couldn't think of anything remotely intelligent to say.

"Speak!" she barked with such harshness that Gunny was pretty sure he saw Agent Grant flinch. "We can't have detectives wandering our streets, talking to people, investigating, can we? What do you have to say for your miserable failure?"

Gunny's mouth felt dry as dust. He tried to swallow but couldn't. The Grand matron's gaze was dreadful, and even though she was much shorter than him, he felt dwarfed by her presence.

Gunny attempted again to speak. “I, uh,” he began before trying again to swallow without success. “I already confronted him. He ain’t gonna be no trouble. I’m handlin’ it.”

The Grand Matron’s voice rose both in volume and pitch. “But what is he *doing* here?”

Since she hadn’t asked directly how Detective Cross had slipped past him, Gunny chose not to volunteer the information and instead said, “He told me he was hunting a stolen car, a Ferrari I think. Probably one of them fancy cars you’re always bringing here. He said it had a GPS tracker in it or something that led him here. But I told him there must be some mistake, and we hadn’t had nothing like that ‘round here. Honestly Miss, he didn’t strike me the trouble-causing type. I think he’ll agree to the rules and do as he’s told.”

Gunny didn’t believe a word of his last sentence, but he didn’t know what else to say. And he couldn’t get out of his mind how the Grand Matron had referred to his “miserable failure.” The last sheriff had gone missing eighteen years ago for reasons he was scared to imagine, and Gunny couldn’t shake the feeling that he was about to be next.

The Grand Matron stared at him in silence for another terrible moment, and then without further interrogation, she stood up and headed for the door in the right wall. Agent Grant followed, opened the door, allowing the Grand Matron to pass through first, and then closed the door behind him. Gunny was left standing alone again in the dimly lit room. If there was a trash can, he was pretty sure he’d throw up. His body was weak all over. He briefly considered sitting in the chair behind the desk, but decided against it.

Several more minutes passed. His stomach informed him it was now well after dinner time. It was probably dark outside by now, but there was no way to be sure from inside this underground room. Gunny was unsure now what to do. Was he supposed to leave? Could he even leave? He assumed the door had locked behind him as he entered. Gunny wished he had gotten his watch battery replaced. He had no clue what time it was or how long he'd been down here. And his cell phone was in his truck.

Finally after what must've been an hour, the door to his right opened again and in came Agent Grant. He sat behind the desk and after a brief pause said, "The Grand Matron Von Druska doesn't share your optimism, but she's willing to see if your word means anything. You're to tell no one about this meeting, not even the Franklin woman at the burger place.

"From now on your shift on the main road will be taken by one of our agents and you're to keep an eye on the detective – without making him more suspicious than he already is. Tomorrow you will tell him the rules. And you will report back directly to me. If you fail us again, or if the detective causes any further trouble, you'll never see him – or your daughter again. Do I make myself clear, Sheriff?"

The mention of Tiffany terrified him. Part of Gunny's agreement with Hive was that he'd do whatever it was they wanted, and they'd leave his daughter alone. Gunny's usual confidence and swagger were gone, so he just nodded and gave a weak smile.

"Good," said Agent Grant. "You may leave. Go home but don't speak of this to your daughter. Tell her you were busy cleaning up a car accident south of town."

And with that, Agent Grant stood and returned to wherever he'd come from. A moment later, Gunny heard a click of the door unlocking behind him.

The drive home was filled with Gunny's thoughts of Hive, Tiffany – and his wife. He wiped back a tear as his truck tires crunched on the gravel driveway leading up to his house. It was pitch dark outside by now except for the porch light that flickered behind the wings of June bugs and moths. He saw the front door open and Tiffany peering out. Gunny grabbed his hat, and headed for the house.

CHAPTER FOUR
RUN!

Tiffany had what seemed like a million questions, but to her dismay, her dad just brushed them off as usual. “Dad, are you sure there’s nothing up – maybe with, you know, Hive?”

“Honey, that’s ridiculous,” Gunny assured her. “Like I told you, there was a bad accident just south of town, and I was helping with the cleanup. I haven’t seen anyone from Hive today, and that’s the way I like it. You know I can’t stand those creepy thugs.”

“Are you sure, Dad? Is everything really ok? I was so worried.” She hugged her dad tightly, not fully convinced. She’d finally forced herself to eat a small snack earlier, so she said goodnight and headed to her room. It was nearly ten and she wanted to be rested up for what she hoped would be a profitable day tomorrow helping Sam with his investigation into the Missing.

As she walked past the hallway mirror, she saw her hair was still up from work. She hadn’t showered since coming home. Cooking burgers and French fries always made her hair greasy, so she headed for the shower before going to bed. Once inside the bathroom, she undressed and then reached up to let down her hair. As she did, she looked at the reflection of her arms in the mirror. She had never been one to work out and now that she was about to go up against an unseen evil, she suddenly wished she wasn't nearly so scrawny. Tiffany sighed and then stepped into the shower, hoping the warm water would wash away the stress of the day.

***

5 hours earlier

Sam walked inside the dated but well-maintained bed and breakfast. From the back room came a woman Sam figured had to be Gena. She looked to be in her sixties, though unusually frail-looking for her age. She froze momentarily when she saw him. *People around here really aren't used to strangers, are they?* thought Sam.

"Evening, sir. Can I help you," said the woman. "I'm Gena Ross, the owner. Will you be needing a room?"

"Yes ma'am. Just one night. Room for one. Ground floor please if possible." By this time, Sam was strongly contemplating an escape attempt after dark, and he didn't want to navigate potentially squeaky stairs in the dark when it came time to sneak out.

"Well right now, you're our only guest," said Gena. "You can have any room you like. We have two on the ground floor: the Cottage Room and the Grand Room. The Cottage Room has its own exterior entrance, but just a half bath. The Grand Room has a full bath, but no exterior entrance; so you'd have to enter here through the front door. The Grand Room, seeing how it's bigger, is ten dollars a night more."

"I'll take the Cottage Room." Sam pulled out his wallet to pay. Having an exterior door to his room would make a late night exit that much easier.

"Just sign here, and you can pay at the end of your stay – or weekly if that's what it comes to." Gena indicated he could pull his car through the side alley and enter his room there if he liked. Sam smiled and thanked her, and headed back outside.

"Oh, Mr. Cross, I mean, Officer Cross," Gena called after him, "will you be needing supper? It's at six. It's included in the price of your room."

"Yes ma'am, that'd be perfect. I'll see you then."

Sam pulled his car down the alley and parked next to the entrance to his room. As he got out of the car, he popped the trunk. One thing he'd been told when he became a detective was to always travel with a "go bag," a small duffel with the necessary items for an overnight stay. "You never know when a routine case will turn into an overnighter," his supervisor had told him on his first day as a detective. Sam was thankful he'd followed that advice.

As Sam headed for his room, he looked back out at the street. Across the road was the Hamlin Public Library. He was being watched. Parked in front of the library was black SUV just like Tiffany had mentioned.

Inside his room, things were nice enough. It was a small room with just the bed, a narrow end table, a sitting chair, a small writing desk and the bathroom. Sam understood why his room was called The Cottage Room. The décor was intentionally rustic, with wood panel walls and a faux wood burning stove. The quilt on the bed reminded him of something you'd see on an old western show. He headed for the bathroom to wash up before dinner.

Sam dried his hands with the towel and looked at the clock. By now he'd made up his mind to attempt an escape. Since he had about thirty minutes before dinner, he sat in the chair to put together a plan. The chair, however, was more comfortable than he anticipated and within moments he was fast asleep.

***

Sam woke up in a dimly lit room. Where was he? How did he get there? And why was his head throbbing? He reached up to investigate the pain in his head only to discover he was in handcuffs, and they were somehow shackled to the chair he was sitting in. As his eyes adjusted to the dim light, he realized he was sitting in a metal folding chair like the one in Sheriff Gunn's office. In fact, Sam wondered if he was being held in a room at the police station. Sam tugged at his shackles, but they only cut into his wrists. As he pondered his predicament, the door to his "cell" opened and in came a Hive agent. The agent slowly removed his facemask and to Sam's tremendous surprise it was Sheriff Gunn.

"What's going on here? Let me go!" shouted Sam.

"You should've listened, Detective," chided Sheriff Gunn. "I warned you about poking around and trying to leave. Instead you had to go and bring my daughter into it. I've already dealt with her. Now it's your turn to join the Missing," Gunny sneered.

"Get away from me!" yelled Sam.

A knocking sound and a voice calling his name woke him from his sleep.

"Officer Cross, it's Gena. Dinner time. Officer Cross? Are you in there?"

Sam reached up to rub his face, thankful that the handcuffs were only in his dream. He breathed a sigh of relief and answered, "Yes, ma'am I'm here. I'll be out for dinner in just a minute." Sam walked to the bathroom sink, splashed water on his face, and headed to the dining room to join Gena for supper.

They ate in silence. Supper was actually quite good. Sam hadn't stayed at a bed and breakfast before so he had no idea what to expect, but Gena's cooking was almost like eating at home. A sudden realization hit him like a ton of bricks: he'd completely forgotten about his wife and two kids. The unfolding events of the day had so filled his mind that he hadn't thought of his family once since several hours earlier at Sheriff Gunn's office. He could just imagine how worried his wife must be. She was well used to the role of a cop wife – the crazy and long shifts, him not always being there at dinner time and bed time, but this was the first time in the thirteen years they'd been married that he hadn't at least called to say good night or texted that he'd be in late due to work. But though his wife was a worrier, he had always admired her faith. It comforted Sam some to know that she would be praying for him.

Gena finally broke the silence. "Sorry for acting funny earlier at check-in. To be honest we don't get many visitors in Hamlin."

"So I've been told," said Sam.

"I'm surprised you didn't change out of your work clothes into something more casual. Do they make Oklahoma City police officers wear their uniform even off duty?" asked Gena.

"It's complicated," answered Sam. "I'm actually a detective and I didn't plan for this to be an overnight trip, so this is really all I've got with me."

"Oh. Well if you need a change of clothes, there's an all-night department store over on Broad Street," said Gena.

Sam smiled and thanked her.

They continued eating in silence for a few minutes when, once again, Gena spoke up. "If you don't mind me asking, and I don't mean to pry, but what brings you to Hamlin?"

Sam thought for a minute how to answer. He considered the possibility that Gena was working with the Hive agent across the street and, like Mrs. Franklin, was trying to pry information out of him."

"Just police business," Sam finally said.

Sam looked up from his dinner and noticed Gena had stopped eating and her hands were shaking.

With a voice as shaky as her hands, Gena spoke as though she was fighting back tears, "Detective Cross, you know I'm not originally from this town."

Sam was at a loss for words. So there were other people like him here in Hamlin that had come here by accident or for some other reason and had been told they couldn't leave.

Gena continued, "Sixteen years ago, that was back before they had people posted on the main road by the edge of town to discourage strangers from coming here, I got turned around, trying to get to the interstate and ended up here by accident. Then I drove over a nail or something and got a flat tire over on

Jeffery Street a few blocks from the city dump. I thought someone might be there that could help me change my tire so I walked over. I didn't mean to snoop, but I called at the gate and no one answered and so I tried looking for a way in, thinking someone might be in that shop inside. That's when two men dressed all in black, faces covered by masks, grabbed me."

"Hive?" asked Sam.

"Yes. And they were so rough and unkind. They took me to see someone they called Agent Grant. For what seemed like hours, they asked me again and again who I was and why I was snooping around town. I tried to tell them I was just looking for help with my car, but it's like they didn't believe me.

"Finally, they told me that so long as I followed the rules, and agreed to never leave town again, they wouldn't hurt me anymore. I've never been so scared in my life and so I agreed. I didn't know what other choice I had. For the next thirteen years, I lived with one of the ladies 'cross town and worked at her dress shop. I finally saved up a little money and bought this abandoned house. It'll be three years next month that I've had this place."

Sam interrupted. "What about your family? Didn't anyone come looking for you?"

"My Tony passed away twenty years ago," Gena replied wistfully. "We'd been married twenty-five years. Kids are all moved away. I suppose someone looked for me, but since I came to Hamlin by accident, nobody would've known to look for me here. I think about my kids and grandkids a lot. Sure do miss them."

Sam hesitated and then confessed, "Seems I've wound up in the same boat as you, though under different circumstances. I came here to investigate a very expensive stolen car."

"So did the agents talk to you too then?" asked Gena.

"No. Just Sheriff Gunn," Sam replied. "But he told me about like that agent told you. That I can't leave. I'm still trying to wrap my brain around that. I've got a wife and two kids that I have to get home to though. I'm sure they are worried sick about me. I was actually thinking about them a few minutes ago. Question for you: did you ever try to leave, you know, at first when they told you that you had to stay?"

"I thought about it," said Gena. "I thought real hard about it. I even made my mind up a time or two to try it one night after it got dark, but fear always got the best of me. And them agents are out there all hours of the night. They're always creeping around town. Sometimes I think they still watch me, even though I've been here all these years. Very untrusting bunch."

That was the last thing Sam wanted to hear. Everything in him urged him to make a run for it tonight but if Gena was correct, there didn't seem to be much hope. And of course, there was the Hive SUV parked across the street at the library, and he didn't know how many others might be on the main road out of town. Just getting his car out of the alley without being seen would be next to impossible.

"Is there any way to get a phone call out of here, you know, to the outside world? Is there any way I could get a call back to Oklahoma City?" Sam asked.

"If there is, I don't know how to do it. I've tried before, but all I ever get is a garbled electronic sound," answered Gena. "I tried everything I could think of without any luck. Maybe someone more tech savvy than me could figure it out, but who knows. Hive keeps a tight lid on things here."

Gena changed the subject. "You know, it's a good thing you decided to stay here instead of at the Freeway Inn. I think Mr. Olsen is in cahoots with Hive. I've suspected for a while that they were paying him to report on folks staying there. Probably got hidden cameras in the rooms and that kind of thing."

"Tiffany recommended I stay here," Sam answered.

Gena gave Sam a playful smile and winked. "Oh she's a sweet girl; smart – pretty too, if you were twenty years younger. Her and her friend Laura both, though I ain't seen Laura the last week or so. Wonder if she's sick or something."

They spent the rest of dinner chatting about family. Though Sam missed his family and was worried for them, it helped to talk about them. After supper, Gena made a pot of coffee. Sam took a cup, thanked Gena for supper, and headed for his room. For the next two hours, Sam sat on the edge of the bed with the light off trying to decide what he should do. Periodically, he'd pull back a corner of the curtain and peek out the window. Each time the black SUV was still there.

Sam prayed for wisdom like he'd never prayed before. Finally, as the clock in his room rolled over to 9:00PM, and he was sure Gena had gone to bed for the night, Sam gathered his things together in his duffle and moved quietly toward the alley door. As foolish as it sounded to make a run for it, Sam had to at least try. He made one final glance out the window. To Sam's relief, he could no longer see the SUV. He hesitated. What if it had just moved to trick him, but was still nearby? Sam went ahead.

Slowly Sam opened the door. He winced instinctively expecting it to creak. Thankfully it didn't. Sam stepped gingerly across the gravel, doing his best to make as little noise as possible. Turns out, combat boots weren't designed for sneaking quietly. Sam grimaced as his every step crunched in the gravel. Using the key instead of the clicker so as to make as little noise as possible, Sam unlocked the driver side door of his car. He tossed his duffle in the passenger seat, closed his door slowly to prevent it from slamming, and started the car.

So far so good, he thought. The car tires crunched loudly on the gravel as he rolled slowly forward, but that was unavoidable. Earlier in his room, Sam had decided to head south out of town, even though the way home was north toward I-40. If Hive was indeed guarding the road, Sam guessed that it would be more heavily guarded in the direction they expected him to run. He chose to drive south on Broad Street because it took him past the department store Gena had mentioned during supper. If he was followed or worse stopped, he could say he was just headed to get some clothes for his stay.

The roads were empty of other cars, so Sam drove with his lights off to draw as little attention as possible. As he drove past the bank, to Sam's dismay, he saw headlights coming in his direction. As the vehicle approached, he saw it was a large pickup. It belonged to Sheriff Gunn's. Sam wondered where the sheriff had been at this time of night and cursed his terrible luck. Sam had no choice but to continue driving and hope Gunny missed him in the dark.

Suddenly about twenty-five yards in front of him, Sheriff Gunn whipped his truck sideways, blocking the road. Sam was forced to slam on his brakes, barely stopping in time. Sam gripped the steering wheel tightly weighing his options. He had hoped to get closer to the edge of town before making his fast getaway. Bolting here in the middle of town brought his chances of escape down dramatically.

Sam decided the best course of action was to sit tight and see what the sheriff would say. Gunny approached the window, and Sam rolled it about halfway down. Gunny shined his flashlight through the window. "Look who it is where he ain't supposed to be again. In the middle of the night no less." Gunny shined his flashlight over on Sam's duffle in the passenger seat. Sam now wished he'd taken the time to put it away in the trunk. "You wouldn't be trying to leave our little town now would you, Detective?"

"Nope, just headed over to the store. Figured if I was going to stay a while, I ought to pick up a couple changes of clothes. Gena told me about a department store that's open all night. And since I couldn't sleep – on account of being held hostage, I decided to pick some things up tonight. And to be fair, 9:00PM isn't really the middle of the night."

Gunny smirked. "They don't teach y'all up in OKC to drive with your headlights on? Mighty dangerous this time of night. Might hit someone."

Sam muttered something about how he must've forgotten and switched them on. Sheriff Gunn gave Sam a final warning about not leaving. "They'll be down there watching the southbound town exit, too. They think of everything. Come to think of it, I'm glad I ran into you tonight. Need you to come by the office tomorrow some time before lunch. There's some rules you need to get down since you're going to be staying here."

Sam gave a weak smile and nodded his head. He watched as Gunny backed out of his lane and headed north, presumably home for the night. *So much for leaving tonight,* thought Sam. He slammed his hand down on the steering wheel. Fine. He'd stay the night, but Sam had no intention of making a new life here like everyone expected. Sam put his car in drive and continued south. Since he'd come this far, he might as well really get some things from the store before heading back to Gena's for what would probably be a sleepless night.

Finally, about 10:15PM, Sam pulled back into the alley at Gena's and entered his room. He crumpled up the note he'd left on the desk saying goodbye and thanking Gena for her hospitality. He undressed, placing his pistol on the nightstand beside the bed, and slid into bed. It wasn't like his at home, but he found it comfortable enough, and despite his earlier doubts, he drifted off to fitful sleep and strange dreams.

CHAPTER FIVE
RENDEZVOUS

Tiffany woke up well before her alarm clock. Perhaps it was from going to bed the night before earlier than normal or just the excitement of what today would hold. She got out of bed and looked in the mirror. Her hair was a wreck from going to bed with it wet. She stared at the reflection of her slender frame. She flexed her arms and stifled a laugh. "Oh well. Good thing Sam is a police officer and has a gun." She knew she wouldn't be much help in a fight.

Tiffany walked over to her closet and stared at its disorganized contents spilling out on the floor, debating what to wear for the day's activities. She opted for black calf-length leggings and an oversized short sleeve grey t-shirt. Instead of the flip-flops she usually wore on her days off, she rounded out her outfit with ankle socks and sneakers. Tiffany figured she might as well be ready to run if circumstances required it. She brushed out her hair and put it up in a lazy ponytail.

Tiffany walked to the kitchen and poured a bowl of granola. Her dad came out a few minutes later.

"You look like you're dressed for taking a hike," Gunny commented as he looked at her outfit.

Tiffany deflected, "Just feel like being alone with nature today. I think I'll go walk around the lake.

Me and Laura used to go there sometimes and skip rocks. No one ever goes anymore, so it's always quiet there."

"Well, watch out for snakes," Gunny said.

Tiffany made an "ew" face. *The Hive should do something useful and make the snakes go missing,* she thought. "Thanks Dad, for putting that thought in my head," Tiffany replied.

She rinsed her bowl in the sink, kissed her dad on the cheek and headed out the door.

"Want me to give you a ride when I head into the office?" Gunny called after her.

"No thanks. I'll walk," Tiffany replied as she closed the door behind her. Last thing she needed was for her dad to run into Sam headed to meet her. It was about a quarter to nine when she was supposed to meet Sam, so she set out with a brisk jog.

***

Sam looked at his watch: 8:00AM. He was supposed to meet Tiffany at the lake in an hour – an appointment he hadn't planned to keep since he'd intended to be gone last night. But the warning of Gena and the run-in with Sheriff Gunn had changed his mind. Sam had come to the conclusion that the only way out of here and back home to his family was to do what he came to do, investigate and solve the case.

He quickly changed into the clothes he'd bought the night before: a pair of dark khaki cargo pants and a loose-fitting grey button up-shirt. He wanted to be able to still carry his service weapon and gear, but keep it easily concealed. Sam joined Gena for breakfast and apologized as he sat down that he'd have to "eat and run."

In between mouthfuls of blueberry pancakes, Sam peppered Gena with as many questions as he could. He once again apologized and promised he wasn't trying to interrogate her.

He started with the missing car. "So have you seen any expensive cars brought into town? The reason I came here in the first place was because a quarter-of-a-million dollar sports car was stolen and I tracked its GPS here."

"Yes sir. From time to time," answered Gena, "though I'm not really into automobiles. But I've seen the occasional fancy one come through every now and then."

That confirmed Sam's suspicion that Hive was partially funding whatever their operation was by stealing and reselling stolen cars, probably overseas.

"I hope I don't offend you with this next question," began Sam, "but what's your opinion of Sheriff Gunn?"

"Oh, no offense taken. Gunny? He's mostly harmless," laughed Gena. "He likes to put on a big show of being tough, but he's a good man. Though I'm pretty sure he helps Hive from time to time with things they tell him to do. But I get the impression he does it because he feels he has no other choice. It's just him and his daughter Tiffany, and Gunny does what he feels he has to do to protect her. But I get the sense he has no love for those ruffians."

"And how well do you know Mrs. Franklin?" Sam asked next.

"Well enough to know she can't be trusted," answered Gena with a hint of spite in her voice. "Don't get me started on that woman. She sticks her neck out for nobody but herself. I don't know where she gets it because her mother, Granny Franklin wasn't like that. Granny was a dear friend before she passed away two years ago. But I wouldn't trust that Mrs. Franklin with a dog I didn't like."

Sam chuckled at that answer. "Well alright then." Sam looked at his watch again. "Shoot, I've got to run." He took one last swig of coffee, thanked Gena for breakfast, and headed for the door. "Don't expect me for lunch," Sam said as he headed out, "and I can't say for sure yet about supper."

Gena waved and Sam closed the door. He walked around the side of the inn to his car. As he reached for the door handle, he caught sight of a piece of paper flapping in the wind underneath his wiper blade. He pulled it out and unfolded it. It was a handwritten note that read:

"Glad you decided to stay.
– Agent Grant"

And stamped underneath the signature was a seal or insignia Sam had never seen before: a grotesque face surrounded by several smaller faces and what Sam thought was a wasp above it. He didn't have to be a world-class detective to put two and two together that this was the emblem of Hive and the note was from the same Agent Grant that had frightened Gena into staying many years ago. Sam's first inclination was to crumple it up, but he decided he'd better hang onto it as evidence.

The black SUV from across the street hadn't returned which was a relief. He started to drive back the way he'd come yesterday from the lake but remembered the Hive SUV that had been parked at the elementary school and decided to take a different route that didn't take him by the school.

Sam arrived at the lake with a minute to spare. He parked in the same place he had the day before and looked around for Tiffany. As eager as she'd been yesterday to help out, he was surprised she wasn't there waving at him as he drove up. Just then the door to the ladies restroom opened and Tiffany came out, her face flushed. Sam got out of his car and walked over to greet her.

"Hi. I was just in the bathroom splashing some water on my face. I was afraid I'd be late, and you'd leave without me so I ran part of the way. It's already so humid out, I was drenched by the time I got here." Tiffany laughed. "So much for the shower I took last night. That's summer in Oklahoma for you. Hope I don't stink." Tiffany's face flushed again, but this time in embarrassment.

"Hey, no problem. I'll just try not to breathe too deeply," Sam said with a grin.

Tiffany rolled her eyes. "So, where should we start?"

"Don't get too excited," replied Sam. "Detective work isn't like you see on TV. It's a lot of asking questions and a lot of observing and a whole lot of patience. I'm as eager as you are to solve this mystery so I can get back home. But we've got to be careful not to make any stupid mistakes.

"Why don't we just sit here under the pavilion a minute and let you air out," Sam said with a wink, "and you tell me everything you know about Hive, about Hamlin, and about the people here."

For the next thirty minutes or so Tiffany relayed all she'd learned in the last week in her own little investigation, and what she knew for as far back as she could remember. Sam listened intently and added a few notes to those already in the pocket-sized notepad he kept. Tiffany gave basically the same profile about Mrs. Franklin that Gena had said earlier at breakfast: not able to be trusted. She told him about various people she could remember that had gone missing. Finally Tiffany told Sam about her interrupted rummage through the filing cabinet at her dad's office. Sam made a note to see if they could get back in and investigate there further. Lastly she told Sam about her dad coming home late last night.

"Yeah I ran into him on my way to the store. He stopped me and grilled me about being out after dark. I think he thought I was trying to leave town." Sam felt bad about lying to Tiffany, but decided not to tell her that he really *had* planned to leave. He didn't want to upset her considering she was so excited to help him in his investigation, and how much she hoped to find her friend Laura.

"You mentioned a records room at the police station. I saw that myself the other day when I was visiting with your dad. I'd really like to get a look in there for myself. I feel like there'd be some useful information to get us pointed in the right direction."

"Well last time I looked in there, it was while my dad was getting us lunch," Tiffany said. "I could probably get a look again the same way, but getting you in would be quite a bit trickier."

"It's not very sophisticated, but if you did the same thing, I could park somewhere nearby and then sneak in as soon as he left. The only hitch is getting back out without being caught." Sam stroked his chin as he thought.

"Also, even though I've agreed to let you help me," Sam warned, "we need to be careful so it doesn't *look* like we're working together. It's okay to meet each other out here for instance, but we shouldn't be seen together. Meeting with you when you're working or 'chance' meetings will help maintain our cover. You'll be what the police call a 'confidential informant.' No one can know that we're working together. Make sense?"

"So, kind of like a spy?" asked Tiffany excitedly.

Sam laughed. "If it makes you happy to call it that, sure. But honestly, it'll help me most if you'll just go about your life as normally as possible and keep your eyes and ears open. Ask questions without raising suspicion and report back to me when we meet."

"And don't take this wrong," Sam added, "but you have a naivety about you that will actually be a help to us."

Tiffany looked a little wounded so Sam explained. "What I mean is that everyone is suspicious of Detective Sam Cross. I've had Hive watching me since I arrived. But you're from here. Nobody suspects you of anything, and that's a huge advantage to us."

Sam could tell Tiffany was disappointed. "Well it's not quite what I envisioned, but I suppose you know what you're talking about. So, I'm supposed to just go to work and stuff? That's so boring."

"Actually today you can help me get into that records room. I really think that's an important place to start looking and learning. What time does your dad take his lunch usually?" Sam asked.

"Oh, just whenever really," Tiffany replied. "Let's see," she said looking at her watch. "It's only 9:45AM. He for sure won't take it any sooner than 11:30AM."

With plenty of time to kill, Sam and Tiffany reviewed what they knew so far. Sam also got a detailed description of Tiffany's missing friend Laura. They'd been friends since kindergarten. Laura was Tiffany's polar opposite. Tiffany was quite slender, with blonde hair, and on the short side – "Five foot two *and a half*," she had emphasized. Laura on the other hand, Tiffany described as being taller, maybe five foot eight with dark brown, almost black hair. Also Laura had a fuller, curvy figure though not exactly chunky. Tiffany said that her friend usually got mistaken for being older than she really was.

Laura had long dreamed of being a psychologist, and it was that dream that drove Laura to try to make her failed escape. Tiffany didn't know much of the details about Laura's disappearance though. Laura had said, "You can't know what I'm planning. I don't want you in trouble. If things go bad…they won't be able to pin anything on you."

At 11:00AM they finalized their plan to get into the record room. Tiffany would drop in and ask Gunny to go pick up lunch and bring it back. "I'll order the wings and the chili cheese fries," Tiffany said. "They always take forever to make, so that'll buy us the most time – I'd say at least twenty minutes."

"Perfect," Sam said. "You watch from the front door and holler as soon as you see your dad's truck."

"Then what? How will you get out?"

Sam thought for a moment. "It'll be tight, but my only shot is while your dad's parking his truck around back. Should take him a minute to grab the food and drinks, and I'll dash out then."

Sam really didn't like that answer, but unless something else came to him between now and then, it was the best he had for now. Since Tiffany would have to walk the nearly mile back to the station, she headed out. Sam hollered a "See you in a bit," and since he'd have about fifteen minutes to kill, he drove back toward Gena's. But halfway there, Sam changed his mind. He remembered the hardware store across the street from the station and figured he'd hang out closer by. That way he could see for himself when Gunny left, rather than trying to time his arrival. Plus, since he first arrived yesterday, Sam had been curious to meet the elusive hardware store owner who kept peaking at him from inside the store. *And ya never know, might find something useful in there,* Sam thought.

Sam turned on Main Street and parked just to the right of the door to the hardware store. Sam turned the car off and headed quickly for the door. He intended to catch the owner by surprise before he could disappear to the back of the store. It worked. As Sam entered the store, the owner looked up and frowned.

"Uh, can I help you?" said the startled shop keeper. "Actually I was just about to lock up and leave for lunch, so you'll have to come back later."

Sam didn't budge. "I'll only be a minute. I just wanted to see if you had a couple items."

"Well, if you'll tell me what they are, I'll get them for you," said the owner.

Sam began to walk down the first aisle, ignoring the exasperated look on the owner's face. "No, I'm fine. I'll only be a minute. Maybe I'll see something else I need while looking around." A few moments later, Sam called out, "So what's your name, friend?"

The shopkeeper tapped his fingernails impatiently on the counter. "It's Jim; Jim Thompson, and are you sure there's not anything I can help you find?"

"No, Jim. I'm just looking."

Sam continued to meander up and down the store aisles, all the while listening for Gunny's truck to rumble away. Sam picked up some zip ties and duct tape. *These could come in handy,* he thought. The store wasn't large and so even with Sam's intentionally slow pace, he saw all of it in less than ten minutes. After adding some sunflower seeds to what he'd already picked up, Sam headed to the counter where the frustrated Jim was waiting. Sam placed the items on the counter and took his time getting out his wallet.

After he paid, despite Jim's urging that he was in a hurry, Sam stood at the counter and began making small talk. Just a moment ago he'd caught sight of Tiffany walking up the steps of the sheriff's office, so he only had to stall a couple more minutes..

"So what's there to do around here?" Sam asked. "I noticed a couple museums. Are they worth checking out?"

"Uh, if you're into that kind of thing, I guess," replied Jim. "Mister, I really do need to be getting to lunch."

Just then Sam saw Tiffany and Gunny head out the front door of the sheriff's office. Tiffany kissed her dad on the cheek and Gunny headed around back to his truck. Tiffany headed back inside, though he could still see her waiting on the other side of the glass door. Sam asked a couple more questions about restaurants until he saw Gunny's truck pull out of the parking lot.

Sam could see a look of relief on Jim's face as Sam thanked him and headed outside. He tossed his purchase in his car and, after looking around to see if he was being watched, jogged to the sheriff's office.

Sam stepped inside and Tiffany reached past him to pull the door shut as she exclaimed, "The record room door is locked! I have no idea how to get inside!"

"Let's not panic," Sam replied. "Maybe there's a spare key in his office desk drawer. Sam and Tiffany rushed down the hall. "I'll check the desk. You look on the shelf. Does he have a key rack on the wall?"

Sam rummaged through the desk drawers doing his best not to make it look like he ransacked it. Every moment they searched increased the feeling of panic knowing Gunny wouldn't be gone long.

Tiffany let out a triumphant yell. "Found it!" Sam turned to see her holding up a brass-colored key on a green lanyard.

"Are you sure?"

"Yes! It's marked 'Records' and everything!"

Sam grabbed the key and rushed back down the hallway while Tiffany ran to the porch to keep an eye out for her dad to return. Sam was in such a hurry that he fumbled with the lock, wasting more precious time. Finally inside, he looked around. There were two file cabinets and a half-dozen cardboard boxes stacked against the wall. Sam decided to check the boxes first. He had Tiffany's phone on with the camera ready. They had decided that was faster than trying to jot down notes and more reliable than recalling from memory: just take a photo of anything that looked interesting or potentially useful and go through the information later.

The first box looked like desk knickknacks from the previous sheriff's time in office. Before Sam set the box to the side, he read the former sheriff's name from the old nameplate: Alan Ramsey. The second box was even more useless than the first: nine baseball gloves. Evidently Hamlin used to have a local ball club. Sam set it aside as well and opened the third box. It too was little more than worthless junk. This was starting to seem like a huge waste of time. So far he'd taken zero pictures and learned nothing useful. "You're wasting time, Sam!" he said under his breath.

Sam opened a fourth box. This one looked more hopeful. It was filled with what looked like mug shots. Sam could tell from the various hair styles and glasses frames worn by those in the pictures that they spanned several decades. Behind each person in the photos was maybe a red flag? He picked up one of the photos for a closer look and immediately recognized the emblem from Agent Grant's note left on his car earlier. This was the jackpot then! These had to be photos of the

Missing. There were hundreds of them stacked in just this one box. On the back of each one were initials and a number.

Sam didn't have time to ponder this further. He had to take pictures. He laid them out in groups of four photos and then held up Tiffany's phone and snapped a picture. He then set those four pictures aside, careful to keep their order and then laid out another and took a picture. Again and again Sam repeated this process, moving as quickly as he could, knowing that time was ticking away. Though surely there was some significance to the initials and numbers on the back of the photos, there simply wasn't time to photograph both sides. Sam did snap the backside of one though – just for reference.

Sam worked like a madman, and to his surprise, he was able to finish the box. Sam meticulously placed the photos back in the box like he found them. He put the box top back on and set it aside.

Sam grabbed the next box. Unbelievably it contained hundreds more photos. Tiffany hadn't exaggerated in the slightest when she said perhaps as many as 1,500 had gone missing. Sam started to pull out the first four pictures to begin photographing them like before, but then put that on hold to take a look in the filing cabinets.

Pulling open the first drawer, he began thumbing through the files. *Nothing. Nothing,* thought Sam as he scanned folder after folder.

Just then Tiffany came running in. "He just turned on the street! He'll be here any minute!"

"Go back outside and stall him at the truck," Sam ordered. "I'll be out in just a minute."

Tiffany hurried back outside and Sam pushed the cabinet drawer closed. He turned around and tripped over the box he'd left on the floor, almost falling. Sam looked at the ground. Dozens of pictures were scattered across the floor from the box he'd left open.

"Son of gun!" shouted Sam. He had moments to get outside and to his car, and now there was a huge mess. He dropped to his knees and began scooping up the pictures. Order didn't matter now. Sam figured he had less than a minute before the sheriff caught him. He put the last picture in the box, replaced the lid and restacked the boxes back the way they were. Sam flipped the light off, and pulled the door closed. *Tiffany's phone!* He pushed the door back open and scooped the phone up off the floor. He slammed the door, locked it, and rushed down the hallway.

Too late! He could see Tiffany's shadow through the glass door. As panic set in, Sam had an idea. He dashed to the restroom and ducked inside. He could now hear Tiffany and the sheriff talking as they drew closer. A second later Sam heard the restroom door handle jiggle.

"Who's in there," Gunny demanded.

Sam flushed the toilet and then opened the door. "Oh, hi Gunny. There you are."

Sam looked over Gunny's shoulder at Tiffany. Her eyes were wide in fear.

"Of course, I'm here. This is my office. What in tarnation are *you* doing here?" Gunny asked.

"You told me last night to come by and talk to you about some 'rules' I think you called them. But since this looks like a bad time, I'll just be heading out.

Food looks good. I think I'll head over to Rivals and get some myself."

Gunny glared at Sam, but said nothing as he left. As Sam walked past Tiffany, he deftly slipped the records room key into her left hand.

Sam stepped outside and closed the door behind him. Never in his life had he been so glad to be outdoors in Oklahoma. He closed his eyes for a second and breathed a huge sigh of relief. That had been *way* too close. All Sam could do was trust that Tiffany could get the key put back without her dad seeing. Sam walked across the street to his car.

***

Tiffany and her dad ate their lunch in tense silence. Neither felt like talking really. Gunny was grumpy over Sam being in his office, and Tiffany was still so shook up over Sam almost getting caught that she was afraid if she spoke her voice would waver or she'd say something stupid. To keep from having to talk, she dove into her lunch. Plus she couldn't stop thinking about the key to the records room. If her dad was to notice it missing, he'd be full of questions. She'd knelt earlier, pretending to tie her shoe, and slipped the key inside her sock.

Gunny broke her train of thought by mumbling something about the wings being good. Tiffany nodded and gave a thumbs up and then returned to her thoughts of the key. *I could spill Dad's drink on him; then he'd have to go to the restroom and clean up,* Tiffany thought. Thankfully she didn't have to do anything that drastic or creative, because her dad dismissed himself to go wash up his saucy fingers in the bathroom.

As soon as he left, she quickly licked the wing sauce from her fingers, dug the key out of her shoe, and hung it on the nail behind the door where she'd found it. Just as quickly, she returned to her chair. "Whew! Glad that's taken care of!" Tiffany's heart was pounding in her chest but she felt relieved.

She finished her wings, sipped the rest of her pop, and said goodbye to her dad. But as she turned to leave, he called her name.

"Hey Tiffany, before you go."

"Yes, Dad?"

She turned and her eyes locked with her dad's. He had *that* dad look on his face. "What was Detective Cross doing here?"

"He said he came to talk to you. He arrived literally a minute or two before you got back. I told him you were gone and that we were going to eat lunch when you got back any minute, and so he said he'd come back later. He asked if he could use the restroom real quick and so I let him in. Then you came back, so I came outside 'cuz I thought you might need help carrying the food."

Gunny stared her down, teasing his mustache with his bottom lip, and said nothing.

"Honest Dad, that's it," Tiffany said as convincingly as she could.

"Alright, but I don't want him left alone in here like that again. I don't trust him. He's too curious for his own good."

"Sorry. I didn't think nothing of it. I won't let it happen again. I love you, Dad. I'll see you later at home. I think I'll head to the park and then maybe over to Mrs. Gena's and see if she doesn't mind me playing her piano for a few minutes."

Gunny waved and off Tiffany went. She felt bad sneaking around and lying to her dad, but she didn't know what else to do. And it wasn't all a lie. She really was headed over to Mrs. Gena's, though probably not to play the piano. She hoped Sam would be there. He still had her phone and she was anxious to see what, if anything he'd found in the records room. If he wasn't at Mrs. Gena's, she didn't know where to look for him – maybe the lake again.

It was about a ten minute walk to Gena's. As she walked, Tiffany thought, *I really need to get a car. All the walking is getting old.* Working at Big-B's a few days a week wasn't making her rich very quickly though. "If only I could get out of this stupid town and get a real job," Tiffany muttered to herself. Unlike her friend Laura, Tiffany hadn't given much thought to what she'd like to do if she ever got out of Hamlin. Mrs. Gena had taught her how to play the piano really well. *Maybe I could be a music teacher somewhere,* Tiffany thought.

A few minutes later, Tiffany arrived at Gena's. To her disappointment, she didn't see Sam's car. She went inside anyway.

"Is that you, Detective Cross?" called Gena from her office.

"No ma'am. It's just me," Tiffany called back.

"Oh, come to play the piano?" asked Gena as she emerged from the office.

"I guess for a minute, if you don't mind," answered Tiffany. "I was actually hoping to catch Sam, I mean Detective Cross, here," she said correcting herself. Since she was supposed to not look like she was working with Sam, she figured she'd better stick to calling him Detective Cross when talking to others.

"Isn't he staying here?" Tiffany asked.

"Yes, dearie, he is," replied Gena. "But I haven't seen him since breakfast. He said he wouldn't be back for lunch, and maybe not supper either. I can leave him a note if you'd like."

Tiffany felt Gena staring at her quizzically. *I guess I shouldn't have mentioned that I wanted to talk to Sam,* Tiffany thought. "No, that's ok. I dunno. Maybe I'll leave a note after I play the piano if he's not back. Thank you." And with that Tiffany headed to the piano.

Mrs. Gena had taught her how to play all kinds of music: classical, ragtime, easy listening. But Tiffany's favorite thing to play for some reason was from the old hymnal that Mrs. Gena always stored inside the piano bench. Tiffany wasn't religious; she just found something peaceful about their simple melodies. She took out the hymnal and opened it up to a random page. The song was "The Old Rugged Cross." She began to play its gentle melody.

Halfway through the first verse, she heard Mrs. Gena begin to hum along. For the next thirty minutes or so, Tiffany played one hymn after another: "In the Garden," "Amazing Grace," "It is Well," and "Abide with Me."

Tiffany was just about to turn to another one when Mrs. Gena interrupted. "If I'm not mistaken, I believe Detective Cross just got in. Did you still need to talk to him?"

Tiffany hesitated trying to think what she should say. She didn't want to talk to Sam where Mrs. Gena could hear her. And Sam had cautioned against making it appear that they were working together.

Tiffany declined. "No, ma'am, never mind. It was nothing. I probably should be going home. Thank you for letting me play your piano. I should come do it more often."

"You're welcome any time," said Gena with a kind smile. "I love to hear you play. You know if you'd practice more, you're not far from being better than I ever was."

Tiffany smiled back. "You're too kind. Thank you again. I'll be seeing you."

"Take a cookie with you," Gena said. Tiffany picked two. Nobody turned down Mrs. Gena's cookies. She thanked her again and left out the front door.

Once outside however, instead of heading home, she dashed around the side of the house to where Sam's car was parked in the alley. She looked around to make sure no one saw her and then knocked gently on what she hoped was the door to his room.

Her guess proved to be correct because from inside she heard Sam call, "Yes, who is it?" She saw the curtain pull back slightly and then after a moment she heard the door unlock and Sam opened it. He looked annoyed, but motioned for her to come in.

"It's not a good idea for you to be coming to my room," Sam said. "Someone might see you. I told you our meetings needed to be secluded and any other encounters needed to appear to be by chance."

"I'm sorry, but you have my phone and I also was desperate to know what you found out in the records room," Tiffany replied

Sam softened some. "Did you get the records room key put back ok?"

"Yep, I did it while my dad was washing up from lunch, so he didn't see me. Did you find anything helpful in the records room?"

"I'm not sure yet. I was just about to get started going through the photos actually. It's probably going to take a while," Sam said.

"Oh, I thought you'd be finished by now. You left my dad's office like an hour ago."

"Yeah, I drove around town a bit to get the lay of things. I spotted a few Hive SUVs. And then finally came here.

"Cool," Tiffany said as she lingered.

"Ok fine, you can help me look at the pictures." He pulled her phone from his pocket. "I found two boxes full of photos of random people. The way they were taken reminded me of mug shots. And there were hundreds of them. Also, in the background of each photo was what I'm pretty sure is the Hive flag or emblem."

"Have you ever seen a flag or emblem associated with Hive?" Sam asked.

"No, but honestly since they creep me out, I've always avoided their agents as much as possible," Tiffany said with a shudder.

"Earlier today I found a note on my car from someone who called himself 'Agent Grant' and it had the same emblem stamped on it as what's found on the flag in each of the photos. So, I'm pretty sure it's the

Hive emblem but thought maybe you'd know for sure," Sam replied.

"Yeah sorry," Tiffany said.

"No worries. Anyway, what I did was I laid out blocks of four photos and then snapped pictures of them with your phone. So what I need you to help me with is as I scroll through the photos, tell me if you recognize anyone. I suspect that they are photos of the Missing. Maybe you can help me confirm that."

Tiffany nodded as Sam pulled up the first picture. "Recognize anyone?" Sam asked.

Tiffany looked closely at each of the four faces in the pictures, but shook her head.

Sam swiped the screen right to go to the next group of pictures. Tiffany shook her head again. Sam swiped again and again, but Tiffany recognized none of the people.

"Does something look 'off' to you about some of their faces?" she asked. "Their eyes I mean. There's a coldness about the way some of them look. Doesn't look natural to me."

Sam swiped back through some of the photos they'd already looked at. It wasn't every picture, but Tiffany was right.

"I'd call it an emptiness," Sam said. "They just seem to be staring blankly or at nothing. I've seen a lot of mug shots in my time as a cop and people always make some kind of a face: sad, scared, angry, mocking – something. I've never seen a single person in a mug shot look like several folks do in these pictures. That's a good catch.

Sam swiped through a few dozen more and still none of them stood out to Tiffany.

"Sorry," Tiffany said. "I know we're a small town, but things are weird here. I probably don't know half of the people who live here. Everyone's afraid I think, and so folks just don't come out and socialize like you'd perhaps expect."

As Sam kept swiping he noticed she was nervously biting her thumb nail. After eight or ten more swipes, suddenly Tiffany grabbed his arm while at the same time inhaling sharply.

Tiffany finally found her voice. "I know that guy! He went missing probably like ten years ago. Oh, what was his name!?"

Tiffany massaged her forehead with her fingertips as she tried to coax her brain to give up the memory. "Fred! Fred the druggist!" she finally exclaimed. "My mom used to walk me and Laura down to the drug store and Fred would give us each a licorice stick."

"What happened to him?" Sam asked.

Tiffany's expression took on a look as if she'd been transported back in time. "He just went missing one day," she said. "After Mom left, Dad didn't take us down there anymore, and so I only saw him when Dad actually needed some medicine. I guess I was seven or eight when I noticed Fred wasn't running the store any more. Mr. Greer runs it now and has for so long, I almost forgot Fred used to. He was such a nice man with a good laugh and kind smile." Her voice trailed off. "I guess he's one of the Missing, huh?"

After a few moments of silence, Tiffany blinked as if returning to the present day. She pointed back at the phone. "I guess let's look at some more pictures."

As Sam swiped through photo after photo, periodically Tiffany would point to one she recognized: Mr. Baker the mechanic, Ms. Violet the librarian, even a man also named Sam who had been a groundskeeper at the city park. And from what Tiffany indicated, the pictures weren't exactly in chronological order, but maybe grouped by decade. For instance, best as Tiffany could remember, Ms. Violet had gone missing before Fred the druggist.

After an hour of these "discoveries," Tiffany was an emotional wreck. It was all she could do to keep from crying. Nearly every swipe revealed another person snatched from her life; people she'd known, talked to, and gone to church with when she was little. A few minutes later, Tiffany waved her hand for Sam to stop. Tears were streaming down her face.

"I'm sorry," she said. "Can we take a break for a minute? I didn't know how hard it would be to look at all the faces of people I once knew."

"Sure," Sam replied. "I'll step out and see if Mrs. Gena has any pop. You want one?"

"That'd be great," Tiffany said. "She usually has some in the fridge. I'll take a cola if there's one."

Sam returned less than a minute later, not really giving Tiffany any time to process the afternoon's revelations. As they sipped their soda, Sam tried to get her mind off of the Missing. "So I heard someone playing the piano earlier when I came in. Was that Mrs. Gena or was it you?"

"It was me," Tiffany replied. "I used to come over all the time with Laura. Mrs. Gena taught us both to play, though Laura never really got any good at it."

"I heard you playing hymns. You play well."

"Yeah, that's what Mrs. Gena says. She said that if I kept practicing I'd soon be better than her, but I don't know. Mrs. Gena has such a lovely touch to the way she plays. The hymns are her favorite, so that's why I played them. I haven't been to church since I was little."

"My family," began Sam, choking back emotion that snuck up on him at the mention of his family. He swallowed and tried again. "My family goes every week. Sometimes I miss on account of work, but my wife and boys never miss unless someone's sick."

"I'm sorry," Tiffany said softly. "I guess I've been kinda selfish. I saw your wedding ring, but I've been so focused on finding Laura that I didn't even ask you about your family. They must be worried sick."

"I'm sure they are, but my wife has a rock solid faith. I'm sure she and the folks at church have been praying for me." It felt good to say that, because Sam knew it was true. Sam cleared his throat. "Anyway, I guess we better get back to work if we're going to solve this case so I can get back home. And if we're lucky, find some of these missing folks too. Are you ready to look at more pictures?"

"Ready as I'll ever be, I guess."

And with a deep breath she looked back at the phone screen. Suddenly her phone rang. Both Sam and Tiffany jumped and Sam nearly dropped the phone.

It was Gunny.

"I've got to answer it or he'll be upset." She took the phone and pressed the green button. "Hello Daddy, what's up?"

"That's what I was calling to ask you. Where're you at?" Gunny asked. "I drove over to the lake and you weren't there."

Tiffany looked at Sam wide eyed, unsure what to say. Sam wiggled his fingers and moved his arms mimicking what was supposed to be playing the piano.

Tiffany smiled and gave a thumbs up. "I got bored of the park," she said. "I'm at Mrs. Gena's. Remember I told you I might come over here to play the piano a while. Hope that's ok."

"Gena's huh?" Gunny grumbled. "Isn't that where that detective is staying?"

"Is he?" Tiffany asked innocently. "I didn't see anyone but Mrs. Gena when I came in. I've just been playing the piano while she hums along from her office."

"Eh, ok. That's fine I guess. I'll see you at the house after a while." Tiffany hung up and breathed a sigh of relief.

"I thought I was caught when he called," Tiffany said. "And what was this?" she asked laughing and mimicking Sam's "piano playing."

Sam laughed too. "Clearly I've never played the piano. But it worked didn't it? Alright back to the pictures, and hopefully no one else calls."

They swiped through several more photos on Tiffany's phone. After a few more minutes, Sam swiped to a picture of Tiffany and a girl with black hair. The previous photo must've been the last one he'd taken in the record room.

Tiffany took the phone from Sam. "Oh that's me and Laura. I forgot that was on there. We took that selfie the day before she tried to leave. I had hoped we'd see Laura's picture in the ones you took at my dad's office. I mean, I know she's got to be one of the Missing, but it would've been nice to have the confirmation."

"Well, there was a nearly full box of mug shots I barely began snapping photos of before your dad came back," said Sam. "And there was a whole 'nother box I didn't even look in that could have contained even more pictures of missing people. How long ago did you say that Laura went missing?"

"Today's Friday, so I guess nine days ago, because it was last Wednesday night she tried to escape," Tiffany replied.

Tiffany looked at the clock on her phone and saw it was nearly 5:00PM. "I'd better be going. If I'm not home by supper, Dad'll be annoyed – well more annoyed than he already is. Also, I've got to be at work at eleven, so I don't know if I can meet with you tomorrow."

"That's fine. I need to do some investigating on my own anyway. I don't know if there's much of anything you can help me with right now. If you think you can, without making her suspicious, maybe see if you can get anything out of Mrs. Franklin. I'll stop in tomorrow for a burger while you're working. See you later. Have a good night."

Sam had Tiffany stay put while he checked outside to see if the coast was clear. He walked out to his car as though he needed something from inside it and looked around as he opened the car door. He made a show rummaging in his car and then closed the door.

Returning to his hotel room, he motioned with a jerk of his head for Tiffany to come. "It's clear. Oh, and you'd better delete those photos from your phone. There'd be no explaining things if they were found on there."

Tiffany nodded and said goodnight and then headed off with a light jog. Sam headed back inside to plan his strategy for tomorrow and also to see what Mrs. Gena was preparing for supper.

CHAPTER SIX
RESOLVE

Sam sat down at the small dining room table in Gena's bed and breakfast to a generous helping of lasagna. It looked *really* good. And Sam said as much.

"You know, you may have missed your calling," Sam joked. "You could probably have the best restaurant in town. Everything you make looks, smells, and tastes fantastic. After I'm out of here, maybe I'll bring my wife back to stay a couple nights – just so I can eat some more of your cooking."

The mention of his wife caused Sam to fight back tears again. He'd only been away two days now, and though he'd been away longer before with the job, it'd never been under these circumstances. The part of his disappearance that upset him the most was how his family was in the dark, probably fearing the worst about him.

Gena interrupted his thoughts, "Get out of here?" she exclaimed. Then in a hushed tone as though someone might be listening, she asked, "You mean to tell me you're planning on escaping?"

"No, not just escaping. I plan to bust this whole Hive thing wide open if I can, solve the mystery of the Missing, and set Hamlin free from the fear Hive holds over it. I want to return Hamlin to the 'small-town USA' city it ought to be." It sounded quite fantastic when Sam said it out loud, but that was indeed what he planned to do.

"Do you think you can?" asked Gena. Her tone sounded doubtful.

"I don't know, but I have to try." Sam was resolute. "It's ludicrous to think that Sheriff Gunn and this Hive outfit expect me to abandon my family and normal life and simply settle into the way of things here. I have no intention of doing any such thing. And besides that, this town has been held hostage by Hive far too long. It's time to do something about it. I swore an oath to serve and protect."

Gena interrupted him, "But you don't know anything about Hive. You have no idea how powerful they are. I don't see how you stand a chance. You'll end up dead or missing."

"I'd rather fight back and fail than surrender without a fight. I intend to do whatever I can to bring Hive down and liberate this town. I can't just do nothing!"

Sam apologized, "Sorry, I didn't mean to raise my voice. It just doesn't feel right to give up."

"No, it's all right," Gena said. "If anyone can do it, I believe you'll be the one. And I'm willing to help in any way I can, though I don't know with what."

"Thanks," said Sam. And then he added, "And this really is good lasagna."

They ate together for a while in silence. Finally Sam spoke up, "Once Hive is brought down, if I'm successful, do you think you'll stay here and run your inn, or will you go back home?"

Gena didn't answer right away. After a moment of thought she said, "I used to dream of leaving, but as strange as it sounds, I've been here so long that this place has become my home. I don't know what I'd go back to. Though it'd be a dream come true to see my grandkids. My, how they must've grown." Once again Gena grew quiet.

"Well, I think I'm going to head to my room," said Sam. "Thank you again for supper and your hospitality. I don't know if you're a praying woman, but if so, I could use all the prayers I can get."

***

Jennifer Cross knelt by the couch in the Cross family living room. Beside her on either side were her two young boys. In each of her hands she held one of their tiny hands as they knelt beside her. She was just about to pray when one of her boys spoke up in a voice barely above a whisper.

"Mommy, I miss Daddy. Do you think God knows where Daddy is?"

Jennifer smiled. "Yes Honey. God knows everything. And God can do anything. Let's ask God to bring Daddy home."

She reminded her boys to close their eyes and then began to pray aloud, "Dear God, please watch over Sam wherever he is. Please, God, bring him home to us safe and sound. Help the detectives looking for him to find him soon."

Her voice wavered with emotion, and she paused momentarily to regain her composure. "And, Lord, if he's lost…or hurt..." Sobs cut her words short. She squeezed her boys' hands and they squeezed hers back. After a moment she took a deep breath and finished her prayer, "Lord, I know You work all things together for our good, and so we trust You with Sam tonight. Give him a good night's sleep wherever he is, and in Jesus' name, Amen."

***

"Yes, what is it, Agent 32?" barked Grand Matron Von Druska as her office door swung open.

"It's concerning the sheriff's daughter. She was seen by one of our agents leaving the detective's hotel room," answered Agent 32.

"Well, that's too bad for her. I guess we'll have to bring her in for a chat. Sounds like it's time for her to join the cause – that is, after I make her regret her foolish indiscretion. Bring her to me at once," the Grand Matron commanded.

"And what of her father? He might not let his daughter go willingly," answered Agent 32.

"Then deal with him if you have to," she snapped.

Agent 32 saluted and closed the door, leaving Madam Von Druska alone. She shook her head in disbelief and then uttered under her breath, "There's always some idiot who thinks the rules don't apply to them."

***

Sam sat on the foot of his bed staring at the wrinkled picture of his wife Jennifer and their two boys that he always kept in his wallet. *This has gone on long enough,* he thought angrily. He'd done enough poking around. Forget investigating tomorrow. It was time to actually do something about getting home – now. The sun was setting and it would be dark soon. Then he'd make his move.

But this time he'd not attempt an escape like he had the night before. He intended to investigate the Hive compound under cover of darkness. But first he needed to make another late-night trip to the store.

During the ten minute drive to the store, he passed what he was pretty sure were two different Hive vehicles: black SUVs parked in inconspicuous places. Once inside the store, he picked out a pair of black pants, a black long-sleeve shirt, and some black shoe polish. These items, together with his police issue black boots and gloves, would make him completely blacked out when it came time to head for the Hive compound. Sam paid for his purchases and headed for the door when coming right toward him were Gunny and Tiffany. Being seen was inevitable, and so Sam braced for a potentially awkward exchange. Sure enough, Gunny locked eyes with him and his face assumed the usual frown the sheriff seemed to always have when he was around.

"Sheriff. Ma'am," Sam said as he attempted to walk by without stopping.

"Hold up," said Gunny. "Wasn't you here just last night?"

"What if I was?" Sam retorted. "It's a free country isn't it?" The irony was not lost on Gunny. He huffed but said nothing further and walked away. Tiffany looked back over her shoulder at Sam, but kept her mouth shut.

Forty-five minutes later Sam was back in his room. He quickly changed into his all-black outfit and smeared his face and neck with the shoe polish.

Luckily there was a waning moon that was little more than a sliver between the clouds. *Being seen should be the last of my worries,* thought Sam. *Just need to watch out for electronic surveillance.*

Sam buckled on his gun belt and headed for the exterior door when he had an idea. His car was probably being watched, but they wouldn't be watching Mrs. Gena's car. He paused for a minute not sure if he should get her involved. But then Sam turned for the interior door instead. *I wonder if she's even still up at this hour?* thought Sam. As he headed into the lobby, he saw a single light coming from the office.

"Mrs. Gena," Sam called out.

A moment later Gena called out from her office, "Yes, Sam? What can I do for you? If you're looking for the oatmeal cookies I baked earlier, they're on the kitchen table."

"That does sound good," answered Sam, "but I actually wanted to ask you a huge favor." Sam added, "You can absolutely say no if you're not comfortable doing it."

Gena walked out of her office and then jumped like she'd seen a ghost.

"Oh my, you scared the life out of me. What's on your face?" asked Gena, a hand on her chest.

Sam had forgotten about the shoe polish on his face. "Sorry, I was just getting to that."

"I need you to drive me somewhere," Sam ventured.

Gena gave Sam a puzzled look. "Isn't your car ok? You can just borrow mine if you like. I'll get the key."

"No," Sam replied. "My car's just fine. I just don't want to be seen driving it. Hive is probably watching it anyway."

Sam hesitated wondering how much he should say. Finally he just spilled his plan. "I've decided that running isn't an option. But I don't mean to stay here forever either. I intend to move on the Hive base - tonight."

At this Gena's eyes got wide as saucers. "That sounds like a mighty bad idea. And I'm not sure what help I could offer you there."

"No, no," Sam said quickly. "I just need you to drive me within a block or so of their base and then let me out. They won't think anything of you driving through town. Do you think you can do that?"

"I don't drive real good at night..." Gena began and then stopped talking, nodded and gave a weak smile. "Sure thing, Sam. Let me just grab my keys and my shawl."

Sam felt bad dragging Mrs. Gena into this, but he really felt like it would make his plan (that he was making up as he went along) have a much greater chance of success. Speaking of his plan, Sam took a deep breath and thought, *Boy, you'd better come up with something good and real quick.* He knew walking up to the base of a secret criminal organization halfcocked was a recipe for disaster.

Gena came back and again smiled weakly and said, "My car's just out this way." As they got in the car, Gena asked, "I don't have a clue where the Hive base is. You'll have to give me directions."

Sam answered, "You know better than you think. The city dump that started all your troubles those twenty years ago – that's the cover for their base. So we need to go there."

"Well, I'll be," said Gena.

"Now what I'll have you do is drive down Jeffery Street, and about a block away, just slow down real slow and I'll just roll out."

"While the car is moving!" Gena exclaimed.

"Maybe you're right. Probably best for me to just duck out while you're at a stop sign."

They drove in silence. Sam could tell Gena was scared. She gripped the steering wheel so tightly her knuckles were white.

He considered his options once he got to the dump. *I suppose I'll have to scout it out for a bit first*, thought Sam. *I need to spot any surveillance cameras or motion sensors. I really hope they don't have infrared or I'm toast.*

A short drive later, Sam could see the dump a hundred yards or so down the road. He pointed at a stop sign at the next intersection. "That stop sign is a good spot to drop me," he said.

Gena wished him luck and just like that, Sam was gone. He watched for a moment as she drove away, turned down the next street, and then vanished altogether. Sam said a quick prayer and then moved in a crouching manner to the ditch on the same side of the road as the dump. Inside the ditch he unholstered his gun and checked the magazine mostly out of nervousness. He'd already carefully inspected and loaded his weapon back in his room. Sam fixed his eyes on the front gate and headed slowly toward the unknown ahead.

***

At the Gunn home, Tiffany tried to engage in small talk with her dad, but he was grumpier than usual ever since they'd run into Sam at the all-night store. Tiffany instead flipped on the TV. About 8:00PM her dad told her she smelled sweaty and that she should get a shower.

Tiffany rolled her eyes, muttered a "Gee thanks, Dad," and headed for the bathroom. She undressed and got in the shower. Her legs were getting a little prickly, so she took the time to shave them. Tiffany was in no hurry. She didn't have to meet Sam early and her work shift wasn't until eleven, so Tiffany took her time enjoying the steamy shower.

Finally about thirty minutes later, the hot water was beginning to fade, and Tiffany shut the shower off. She reached over to the toilet seat to get her towel – only to realize that she'd forgotten to bring one.

Tiffany stepped out of the shower, dripping as she went, careful not to slip and cracked the bathroom door open. She peeked her face out and called for her dad. There was no answer. *Strange,* thought Tiffany. *Where could he have gone?*

"Daaaad!" Tiffany called out again louder than before, and it was then she heard the squeal of the sliding glass door to the back porch. She waited a second for her Dad to respond, but when he didn't, Tiffany called out again, this time with a distinct annoyance in her tone.

Suddenly around the corner of the hallway came a man dressed all in black wearing a mask. Tiffany screamed. She slammed the bathroom door as the man in black lunged for the handle. The door stopped on something and she heard a loud curse. Looking down she saw that there was a hand in the door. She gave the door a hard shove with her hip and shoulder, smashing the door on the man's hand again eliciting a loud "Ouch!" followed by another string of curse words. She went to slam the door again but this time the hand retracted, and she was able to fully shut it. She fumbled with the lock and after a second was able to lock the door.

Outside the door the man was still cursing. "If you broke my finger, I'll kill you," the man spewed angrily.

A thousand thoughts ran through Tiffany's head. *Was this a burglar? Where was her dad? Was he alive?* She looked at the bathroom door and knew it wouldn't hold long if the man tried to break his way in.

Tiffany glanced around for something to defend herself with. Her eyes fell on the lid to the toilet tank. She snatched it up, sending her body spray bottle that was resting on it flying into the tub.

"Don't you dare come in here!" she shouted through the door. "Take whatever you want. Just don't hurt us!"

Her heart skipped a beat at the sound of a wicked laugh on the other side of the door. "I plan to. And it's your lucky night, because it's you I want," the man said with a devilish tone.

Tiffany screamed again and now tears streamed down her face. Who knows where her dad was. She tried not to think it, but unwelcome images of her dad lying dead somewhere in their house flood her mind. And here she was locked in the bathroom, naked, with only a porcelain toilet lid to protect herself.

"Come out, come out," the man taunted devilishly. "There's someone who wants to meet you."

Meet me? thought Tiffany. And that's when it dawned on her. The intruder was a Hive agent. And for whatever reason he'd been sent to kidnap her. That was little comfort, but it was better than being violated by an intruder which was what she had feared.

Tiffany forced back her tears and said with a shaky voice, "I'll come with you. Just give me a second to get dressed."

Putting back on her old clothes without first drying off proved to be more time consuming than she thought it would be. After a moment there was a loud bang on the door. "Let's go!" shouted the man impatiently.

"Ok, I'm coming out," Tiffany said nervously as she pulled her shirt over her head, and then reached down to unlock the door. As she did the handle suddenly turned and the door burst open. She screamed again and jumped back. The man walked slowly and ominously forward. Tiffany lunged for the toilet lid she'd set down to get dressed, but the agent swung his open hand swiftly across her face.

Tiffany staggered and almost fell into the tub. Her face stung and her ear rang loudly. She grabbed the shower curtain to catch herself, causing the whole thing, rod and all, to come crashing down. Tiffany began sobbing uncontrollably. "That's for smashing my hand," said the man angrily. He raised his hand again, but then stopped. "I ought to give you another one since you smashed my hand twice, but I doubt you could handle it – and then I'd have to carry you to the car.

The man jerked sidewise with his head and said gruffly, “Get moving. The boss doesn’t like to be kept waiting.”

Tiffany straightened up and slowly inched her way forward. The Hive agent leered at her with a disgusting grin. In the bathroom mirror she caught a glimpse of her face. She could see a deep red handprint from being struck. Already there were tinges of purple beginning to appear. When she was about even with the man, she darted by. As she did the man made a lunging motion as if he’d grab her, bringing another scream from her lungs. The man laughed wickedly. “Boy, I love my job.”

As they entered the living room, Tiffany stifled a cry. Her dad was lying motionless on the floor. She started to reach down for him, but the agent pulled her roughly away by the shoulder.

“He’ll be just fine in an hour or two. He’ll have a wicked headache though when he wakes,” the agent said.

Tiffany was allowed to slip on her tennis shoes before being led outside to a waiting black Hive SUV where she was shoved into the backseat. There on the floorboard was a metal ring with handcuffs and chains attached to it.

“You like jewelry, don’t you?” the agent said and laughed again. “I wasn’t going to shackle you up, but after the way you smashed my fingers, you can ride back to the base in full shackles.” He first cuffed her feet. Running up from the ankle cuffs was a thick chain with another pair of cuffs at the top. These he put roughly around her wrists. And then, even though they were plenty tight, he gave the cuffs another click, causing them to dig into her skin and eliciting a sharp cry.

"I guess I'm the vengeful kind," the agent said, "because that's also for smashing my fingers." Now that she was shackled, the agent ran his fingers gently down the red and purple handprint on her cheek. His hand paused at her neck as though it would go lower, but then he suddenly pulled away.

"You're not worth the trouble, or I'd help myself," he said with a sneer and then slammed the SUV door closed.

The way the shackles were arranged, Tiffany couldn't sit all the way back in her seat. Instead she was forced to remain hunched over with her forehead leaned up against the seat in front of her. This meant as they drove, every bump caused her head to bounce painfully against the seat. It also meant she couldn't see at all where they were going.

Hi!

Thank you for purchasing a signed copy of ***The Missing***!

I hope you enjoy reading my book :)

And if you do would you please consider leaving a review on Amazon?

Thank you!

- *Stephen Zimmerman*

CHAPTER SEVEN
INFILTRATION

Sam re-holstered his weapon and began to creep forward. Just then tires squealed and the flash of headlights blinded him. He flung himself flat to the ground trying to hide from the glare. He blinked rapidly. His night vision was ruined and bright white spots danced before his eyes. From the ground he peeked up to see that it was a Hive SUV coming his way.

Are you kidding me! Sam thought. *I've barely begun, and they've found me already. Must've triggered some kind of sensor.* But before reaching his location, the SUV slowed and turned into the short, sloped gravel driveway outside the dump. Sam crawled closer, careful not to make a sound.

An agent exited the front of the driver's side and walked up to the gate. Moments later, the gate slid silently open and another Hive agent walked out. They talked for a minute, though Sam was too far away still to hear their conversation, and then they walked together to the rear passenger door. As they opened it, Sam noticed a slim figure inside, but couldn't make out much more. *Must be their newest addition to the Missing,* thought Sam as he continued to creep forward. He could now hear a female voice protesting but he couldn't quite hear what was being said.

He saw one of the agents reach for his side as though going for a gun, and Sam unholstered his weapon in case he had to defend the captured person in the car. But then Sam saw that it wasn't a gun the agent reached for but a flashlight. Sam still held his weapon ready just in case.

The agent clicked on the flashlight and shined it into the car. The flashlight glinted on a set of shackles and Sam watched as they loosed their prisoner. The woman struggled, but when one of the agents raised his hand threatening to strike her, she stopped fighting.

The entire time Sam had been inching closer and closer until now he was about thirty feet away. If he had to take a shot, he felt pretty good about his chances of striking his target, even in the dark.

Now that he was closer, Sam was able to hear some conversation. The agent who had exited the compound to meet the car said, "Alright, I've got her, go ahead and take the SUV inside to the garage. I'll take her from here."

The SUV driver replied, "She's a feisty one. Keep a good grip on her and don't be afraid to give her a good whack if she gives you too much trouble." He then returned to his vehicle and proceeded through the gate.

The woman prisoner had been re-shackled at the hands and feet with a connecting chain running between them forcing her to proceed slowly forward with an awkward shuffle.

"You know, I could walk a lot better," said the captive woman, "if you didn't have me chained up like a criminal."

It was all Sam could do not to gasp aloud. He recognized Tiffany's voice. Sam abandoned his plan of surveillance, and while still maintaining silence, closed in on the pair.

Sam re-holstered his weapon and removed his police baton from his belt. He waited until Tiffany and the guard were just inside the gate and then stepped silently in behind them.

The guard paused at a small control panel to close the gate and that's when Sam made his move. With a soft clicking sound, Sam snapped his wrist, causing the baton to extend to full length, and before the guard knew what hit him, he fell to the ground with a thud.

Tiffany saw the movement of the guard falling out of the corner of her eye and stumbled to the side, almost falling herself. As Sam emerged silently from the shadows Tiffany stifled a scream but he motioned for her to stay silent. Reaching in his pocket, he pulled out a handcuff key.

Sam leaned near her ear and whispered. "Shhh! It's me, Sam. Let me take these handcuffs off."

Tiffany breathed a sigh of relief and waited as Sam first loosed her ankles and then her hands. As the shackles fell away, Tiffany leaped into his arms with an almost suffocating hug. Tiffany began to whisper to Sam, but Sam held up a finger to his lips and said, "Not now. We've got to get you safely out of here."

"How did you know I was here," whispered Tiffany anyway.

"I didn't. I was coming here to sneak inside when I saw you being brought in and so I rescued you.

But more about that later. Let's get you to safety. I'll take you to Gena's."

"No, I'm ok. Let me help you. That was the plan."

"That wasn't at all the plan. The plan was for you to help me by being my eyes and ears and getting me answers. I didn't say anything about you putting yourself in harm's way."

"I'm already *in* harm's way," insisted Tiffany. "I was just attacked in my own house and kidnapped!"

Sam motioned with his hand for her to quiet down. They stood there for a moment and then Sam finally answered. "Fine, I suppose two sets of eyes are better than one. But we've got to get you disguised."

Sam first turned his attention to the unconscious guard. From his cargo pocket he pulled out the roll of duct tape and some zip ties he'd bought yesterday. Quickly, Sam bound the hands, feet, and mouth of the guard and then pulled him outside the gate and threw him into the ditch where he would be less likely to soon be discovered.

Tiffany whispered, "We should check his pockets. He might have something helpful to us." Sam nodded and together they went through his pockets. Tiffany found a large folding knife which she clipped onto her waistband and Sam found another pair of handcuff keys and a white keycard, both of which he took.

He gave the extra handcuff keys to Tiffany and said, "Hide them on you – like you did the records room key." The only other items in the guard's pockets were some cigarettes and a lighter. Sam took the lighter, because "You never know." Sam had also suggested that Tiffany take the guard's ski mask to hide her face making her blend into the shadows better. She also took the agent's jacket.

Back inside the compound, Sam pushed the green button on the control panel and the gate slid silently closed. Sam picked up the guard's rifle and slung it across his back and handed the guard's flashlight to Tiffany.

"Don't I get a gun?" whispered Tiffany.

"Do you know how to use one?" asked Sam.

"Yes, I've shot my dad's guns several times. He has of course his service revolver and also a hunting rifle. I've shot both."

"Good," said Sam. He unslung the rifle and handed it to her. As he did, he warned, "Don't shoot anything unless I tell you. One gunshot and this whole place will be swarming with agents. Only shoot if I shoot or to save your life. Until then let me use my baton."

"What about to save *your* life?" asked Tiffany.

Sam repeated his instructions, "Only to save your life."

Tiffany nodded and they crept forward into the darkness, making sure to stay out of the various security lights along the side of the building. As they moved, Sam instructed Tiffany to keep an eye out for any surveillance equipment. But to Sam's surprise, they didn't see any cameras or other security devices. Perhaps Hive had the town so in fear that they never anticipated any kind of infiltration or resistance.

They quickly realized that the "junkyard" was not a junkyard at all and that it was far bigger than it appeared from the outside. Ahead and to the left was what looked from the outside to be the salvage yard office, though Sam was now sure that was just a cover for something else. Also ahead but to the right, about fifty yards away, was a large hangar style building. Sam decided to head for the “office.”

Just as they stepped out of the shadow of the gate to head toward the office building, a door opened on the further away “hangar” building, casting a beam of light into the yard. Sam pulled Tiffany to the ground, and they lay there silently. An agent headed their way but didn’t yet seem to be aware of their presence. The agent turned and Sam realized he was heading for the same building they’d been going to. He briefly considered knocking him out in the same way he’d taken out the other guard, but decided that if he started taking out too many guards unnecessarily, someone would notice them missing.

Sam and Tiffany lay in the sunbaked dirt trying to quiet their breathing until the guard disappeared around the left side of the building. After another moment, Sam motioned for Tiffany to rise and together they crept across the open courtyard. Once they reached the building, they sneaked along the side of it in the direction the guard had gone. At the corner of the building, Sam motioned for Tiffany to hold in place. He once again extended his baton, took a deep breath, and peeked quickly around the corner and then pulled his head back. As best as he could tell, it was clear. The guard was nowhere to be seen. Sam took a longer, second look to confirm and then motioned for Tiffany to follow him.

Just around the corner of the building was a single door with a red light above it. Sam gently pulled on the handle, but it didn't budge. To the right of the door was a button, but he decided against pushing it. He looked around and spotted what looked like perhaps a keycard panel on the left-hand side.

Sam reached in his pocket and pulled out the keycard they'd looted from the guard. He looked at Tiffany and shrugged, and then waved the keycard in front of the panel. This elicited an almost inaudible click from the door and Sam motioned for Tiffany to try and see if it would open. It did.

Sam considered the possibility that using the keycard and opening the door might have signaled their presence, but it was a risk they had to take. They stepped inside. Ahead of them lay a single staircase dimly illuminated on the sides by red lights. Sam could just make out another door at the bottom of the stairs.

Sam whispered, "I don't like this at all. If someone comes in behind us while we're on these stairs, we'll be trapped. We now know we can get in here with the keycard, so let's check out that other larger building first." Tiffany whispered an "Ok," and back out the door they went, careful to close it silently behind them.

Now they had to cross the courtyard again, but this time the distance was much further. If someone exited either building while they were crossing the courtyard, there'd be nowhere to hide. Sam whispered to Tiffany, "Do you think you can make a run for it – to that building over there?" Tiffany nodded and off they went. To Sam's surprise, Tiffany outpaced him and reached the building several seconds before he did.

Tiffany grinned. "You ok, old man?"

Sam smiled back. It felt good to smile in such a tense situation. It helped calm his nerves. Once again, Sam peeked quickly around the corner and when he saw it was clear, beckoned for Tiffany to follow. As with the other building, as best as Sam could tell, there was just one door in the wall – though since this building was much longer, Sam couldn't rule out the possibility of a second door farther down. However, unlike the door on the previous building, this one had a small glass window in it through which Sam was able to look inside.

It wasn't a hangar after all, but rather a humongous garage. Inside he could see what very likely the missing Ferrari in addition to dozens of other expensive cars: Corvettes, BMW's, Mercedes, various classic cars, and even a Rolls Royce. Clearly Hive had been quite busy with their car theft scheme. And it was also obvious what they were doing with them. In the center of the room were several large shipping containers into which workers were loading the cars to be sold overseas on the black market.

Sam couldn't see the entire inside of the building through the small window, but in the portion he could see, he counted at least a dozen people. Some were agents and others were simply workers in drab grey jumpsuits. Sam motioned for Tiffany to come forward and whispered, "Look inside and see if you recognize anyone."

Tiffany peered through the small window for a long time, waiting for each person to turn their face in her direction. Finally Tiffany answered, "I think I recognize one or two, but I don't know them personally. It could be that I just recognize them from the pictures earlier today."

Sam suddenly asked, "You deleted those pictures, right? They weren't on your phone when they captured you were they?"

"Yes, I deleted them," replied Tiffany. "But no matter; when that agent took me, I didn't think to grab my phone, so it's back at the house."

Sam looked inside again and after a couple minutes whispered, "There are too many people in there. Unless we can find another, less conspicuous way in besides waltzing through the front door, we're going to have to go back to the other building."

Sam checked the time on his watch. There was still plenty of darkness left so he told Tiffany that he'd wait here by the door with his baton in case someone came out while she walked the perimeter of the building to look for an alternate way in. Tiffany nodded.

***

Tiffany gripped her rifle tightly and walked quietly ahead, her heart was pounding and her mind racing. *What if I stumble across someone and they see me?* she thought.

She wasn't sure she had it in her to pull the trigger. She'd fired plenty of guns before with her dad, but, of course, never at a person. *I guess we'll find out if my life is in danger,* she thought. Tiffany was disappointed in herself at how she'd responded to the Hive intruder. She had never been in that kind of peril before and so she really hadn't given much thought to how she would react in a situation like that, but looking back, she was embarrassed that she'd done little more than scream and cry.

Then she remembered smashing the agent's fingers in the door – twice. *That did feel good,* she thought, grinning. At least that, along with her grabbing the toilet lid, proved that she had the strength to protect herself. And so, if it came down to it now, she determined to fight back again.

***

Meanwhile Sam waited impatiently back by the door. Almost immediately he regretted sending Tiffany off on her own. What if something happened to her? Minute after excruciating minute passed and still Tiffany did not return. Finally, just when Sam had nearly made up his mind to go after her, she rounded the front corner of the building next to the door.

"What took you so long?" Sam asked anxiously. "Is everything alright?"

Tiffany panted, a look of excitement on her face. "I'm fine – but you'll never guess what I found."

Sam stared at Tiffany, waiting for her to catch her breath.

"Well aren't you going to ask me what I found?" Tiffany asked.

"I was just waiting until you were ready to tell me," answered Sam. "Ok so what did you find?"

"This is going to sound crazy, but behind the building is a wall; or what looks like a wall, but it's not real."

"Not real? A wall that looks like a wall, but it's not? You're not making any sense."

"I don't know how else to explain it. You're just gonna have to see it for yourself. The wall is an illusion or a hologram or a projection or something like that. It looks real and you can't see through it, but you can walk through it. And there's like a whole other city, a world almost, on the other side. I only stayed for a second, but it felt like I stepped into another dimension."

Sam shook his head. He'd never heard of such technology. "That's impossible," he said.

"I told you it sounded crazy and that you needed to see it for yourself. It's the most – it's just – like wow! On the other side, there were drab grey buildings, maybe five or six stories tall – maybe apartments, all lined up all in neat rows. I don't know for sure. Again I only stayed for a brief moment. Oh, there was what looked like a launching pad or landing pad of some sort. I'm serious; it looked like something aliens would land on."

Sam believed Tiffany had seen *something* but no way it was as she described. "That's ridiculous," Sam answered. "And you're right. I've got to see this for myself. Let's go. Lead the way."

***

Agent 32 had been drinking a cup of coffee in the breakroom when the watch on his wrist vibrated and the Hive symbol on the screen illuminated red. This was the Grand Matron's way of summoning agents to her quarters.

Aware of the repercussions if he were to arrive late, he quickly stood, took one last gulp of his coffee, straightened his uniform, and walked briskly to meet with the Grand Matron.

The Grand Matron's quarters were across the compound and downstairs next to the armory. A couple minutes later, Agent 32 knocked on the Grand Matron's door and waited for a reply.

"Enter," came the Grand Matron's voice through the door a moment later.

Agent 32 entered the room, stood at attention, and waited for further instructions.

"You have the girl?" asked the Grand Matron without looking up.

"She should have been in holding for a good while now," replied Agent 32. "I handed her off to Agent 19 at the gate. He said he would handle her from there and instructed me to park the SUV."

"Very well," said the Grand Matron. "Did she come without too much trouble?"

"I had to put the sheriff to sleep, but it was no trouble," answered Agent 32.

The Grand Matron looked up and motioned toward the agent's swollen hand. "And that?" she asked.

"It's nothing," replied Agent 32 stoically. "I briefly underestimated the girl's resolve. But like I said, it's nothing and she's in custody. Will there be anything else, Madam?"

"That is all. Let Agent Grant know that I'll join him shortly to go and talk to the girl. You're dismissed."

And with that the Grand Matron turned again to the chart on her desk. Agent 32 saluted and closed the door behind him, heading for Agent Grant's office.

***

Captain Durant of the Oklahoma City Police Department turned his blinker on and prepared to exit the interstate for the small two-lane highway that would lead him into Hamlin – the hopeful destination of Detective Cross. It had been a chaotic last day and a half. The desk sergeant had phoned him mid-afternoon on Thursday to pass the news that Detective Cross hadn't checked in for quite some time. The last transmission from Detective Cross was that the signal to the stolen Ferrari seemed to be south of the interstate and that he should be closing in soon. It was now almost midnight on Friday and Cross hadn't been heard from in over thirty-six hours. *Cross may be a new detective,* thought the Captain, *but he's no rookie cop. If everything was okay, he'd have checked in for sure by now.*

Once the desk sergeant had told him of Cross's radio silence, Captain Durant had jumped into action. It had been nearly eight years since his unit had lost an officer in the line of duty, and the thought of losing any cop, much less a solid guy like Cross with a family, filled him with a deep sense of dread. He'd radioed Cross's former partner to see if he'd heard anything, but nothing. Captain Durant had hated to alarm Mrs. Cross, but as the afternoon wore on, he'd had no choice but to make the call. It had been one of the most difficult calls he'd ever made. She hadn't heard from her husband either, and the news that he hadn't been heard from by *anyone* in several hours had not gone over well. Before Captain Durant had ended the call, he'd given Mrs. Cross his word. "Ma'am don't you worry. I'll see to it personally that Sam is found and brought home. You have no idea what I can unleash when there's an officer in distress."

Durant had called the Highway Patrol to see if any of their troopers had spotted Cross's cruiser, but to no avail. He'd then taken out a map and a phone book and called every city police department along the route between Oklahoma City and the Colorado state line for fifty miles in every direction. But not a single one had reported seeing Cross or an OKC cruiser. He'd put out an "all-points bulletin" for Cross – which meant hundreds of Oklahoma police officers right that minute were looking for any sign of him.

Still, Captain Durant had decided to look for Cross himself. He'd called his girlfriend to let her know that he wouldn't be seeing her that night, and he'd jumped in his cruiser and pointed it toward the highway. That was two nights ago. He'd stopped in upwards of twenty different towns since Cross had disappeared. Though Captain Durant was exhausted from getting barely five hours of sleep the night before – in his cruiser no less, now at this late hour, he turned his car toward one final place before calling it a night: the town of Hamlin. It had crossed Captain Durant's mind that finding a small-town sheriff this time of night might not be possible, but his GPS had told him that Hamlin had a hotel, so he'd spend the night if need be.

Thirty or so minutes later, Captain Durant spotted flashing lights ahead in the road. He slowed as he approached the mess of a pretty nasty traffic accident. A car's bumper lay in the road, along with some glass from two mangled vehicles blocking the roadway just ahead. As he rolled to a stop next to the bumper, an officer walked toward his vehicle. Captain Durant rolled down his window.

"Evening sir," said the officer. "What brings you this way? Hope you're not in a hurry. Road'll be blocked for the next few hours, with cleanup, sketches, and the like. I'm sure you know the drill."

"Yeah, seen it too many times myself," answered Captain Durant. "Quick question for you. I'm looking for one of my officers, a detective actually, who may have come out this way. He's been missing for a day and half, and I couldn't bring myself to just sit and wait, so I'm out beating the streets. Any OKC officers been through town in the last couple days?"

"Wish I could help," answered the officer, "but we haven't had nary a visitor in a week probably. Not many folks come this way. Nothin' much to see or do here. Sorry sir."

"Eh, don't sweat it. It's the same answer I've gotten in the last twenty towns. Say, that looks like a pretty bad accident. Folks make it?" asked Captain Durant.

"Yeah. Miracle actually," answered the officer. "Both drivers pretty much walked away. Hey, I hate to cut you short, but since I guess I can't help you, I'd better get back to the accident. Again, I feel bad turning you away, but it'll be a while before the road is open and it's getting mighty late."

"Yeah speaking of late," yawned Captain Durant, "I was sure hoping to spend the night in the hotel here."

"That's a shame," said the officer. "Old Mr. Olsen over at the inn would've been happy for the business. Problem is, it's on the opposite side of town as you're leaving out the other way. And like I said, it'll be a while before you can get through. I know it's late, but it'll be faster if you head out back the way you came and go down the interstate to the next hotel. Good luck to you, brother. Oh and if I hear anything on your missing detective, I'll phone ya."

Captain Durant reached in his console. "Well here's my card then. Good luck on the cleanup. Stay safe. Have a good one." Captain Durant rolled up his window, pulled a three-point turn, and drove back up the road the way he'd come. He reached over to the map in the passenger seat next to him and put a red X through Hamlin, and then accelerated toward the interstate.

The officer turned to the others and barked, "Alright, coast is clear. Agent 83, report in to Agent Grant."

***

Sam followed Tiffany down the side of the hangar building, carefully watching for any traps or security devices. About five feet behind the building stood a cinder block wall about eight to ten feet tall. To Sam, nothing looked "fake" or holographic about it. Tiffany kept walking right toward it. But instead of face-planting into the wall as Sam expected, she simply passed through it with a faint shimmer and out of sight.

Sam couldn't help himself and let out a low whistle. If he hadn't just seen it with his own eyes, he'd never have believed it. In fact, he still wasn't sure that he did, but then Tiffany's head poked back through the wall and she asked, "Sam, you coming?" And then, poof, she was gone again.

Sam took a deep breath and walked forward, one hand in front of him, expecting to run into a solid wall. But instead of striking brick, his hand went through it. As his body passed through the wall, he held his breath half expecting it to hurt, but without even the slightest sensation, Sam watched a new world emerge in front of him and the familiar old one disappear from sight behind him.

"My God!" exclaimed Sam. "You weren't kidding in the least, unless we're both having some kind of shared hallucination or something."

Tiffany giggled. "Crazy isn't it?"

Sam shook his head amazed. "*Crazy* doesn't even begin to describe this."

He surveyed his new surroundings. It was nighttime here as well, but there were streetlights every few feet which gave off a gloomy yellow, orange glow that, though they illuminated this new portion of the world fairly well, gave Sam a feeling of dreariness and an almost depressive mood. To his left about seventy-five yards or so away was what Sam figured to be a helipad. Behind it, another forty to fifty yards was a runway with a small private jet parked at it. Strangely, the ground in front of him was devoid of grass. What ground wasn't covered in concrete walkways was barren – almost desert-like. The concrete and bare earth added to the bleakness and sterility of the place.

As Sam's eyes wandered down the concrete path, he saw walkways branch off to the left and the right with apartment buildings just as Tiffany had described. They were made out of the same grey concrete as the walkways that led up to them. Sam counted the windows going up, and they seemed to be six stories, but it was hard to tell. The building's windows were dark, but Sam wasn't sure if it was because they were blacked out or simply unlit.

There was row after row of these nearly identical buildings about four rows deep. Beyond them the concrete walkway continued for roughly half a mile where it forked into a "T." From this branch, to the left, the walkway continued to the entrance of a large oval shaped building that reminded Sam somewhat of an enclosed sports stadium. The other walkway leading to the right ended at a second larger building, this one more factory-like, complete with large smokestacks.

Tiffany interrupted his thoughts. "What do you suppose this place is? And what are those two huge buildings in the distance?"

Sam ventured a guess. "I think the one on the right is some kind of factory. And if I didn't know any better, I'd say the one on the left is a sports stadium, but I'm guessing that no one here is playing sports. And you might be right about these closer buildings – they very well could be apartments or dorms. If that's the case, from their size, I'd wager that they could house thousands; though who they're built for, I couldn't begin to guess."

"Maybe Hive agents?" mused Tiffany.

"I sure hope not," replied Sam. "That'd be at *ton* of agents."

Then they both asked the same question nearly at the same time, "Maybe they're for the Missing?"

At the thought of the Missing and her friend Laura, Tiffany began to walk forward, but Sam pulled her back. "Not just yet. I want to investigate the hologram wall we just came through first."

Tiffany sighed in frustration, but Sam returned in the direction they'd come. From this side of the illusions, instead of looking like a wall, it looked like a razor wire fence.

"I'd really like to know how this thing works," Sam said. "And then before venturing any further, we should probably check out that first building with the staircase too."

Sam stepped back through the fence, and again he expected pain of some sort, especially considering the razor wire appearance. But as before, the pass through was painless and without sensation. Tiffany followed.

Back inside the compound, Sam looked to the left and then to the right. The "fence" extended as far as he could see in either direction. Sam chose to head to the right first. They crept along in silence until they came to another cinder block wall in front of them. Sam again put up his hand, not sure it was real or another illusion, but as his hand collided roughly with the wall, Sam realized this one was indeed real. He reached to his right where the fake wall was and his arm passed through as before. *So just this one back wall leading to the grey town is fake,* he thought.

Sam looked up and down the real wall, but saw no projection device of any kind that could explain the illusion. Sam motioned to Tiffany with his head to go back the way they'd come and they walked a couple more minutes back past the hangar building eventually to another wall. Sam reached up again and as he felt it with his palm, he discovered, as he expected, that it too was real. Once again, he inspected the real wall, but still found no evidence of any kind of technology to explain the fake wall now to his left.

"Craziest thing I've ever seen," whispered Sam.

"I know," Tiffany whispered back. "What do you suppose is making the fake wall?"

Sam frowned and shrugged. "I haven't the foggiest idea."

CHAPTER EIGHT
DISCOVERED

Agent 32 walked away from the Grand Matron's office and headed to find Agent Grant. As he walked, he flexed his sore hand from being smashed in the bathroom door at the Gunn house. Though he'd concluded that it wasn't likely broken, it still hurt a ton. "I hope I get a minute alone with that stupid girl," he thought angrily. "I'll make her regret this for the rest of her miserable life, or at least until she joins the rest of the workers."

Agent 32 walked down the long winding corridor and finally arrived at Agent Grant's office. He knocked sharply twice and then waited for a response. None came. He knocked again. Still no response. He tried the handle to the door. It was locked. Agent 32 cursed under his breath, spun on his heel, and made his way to the building's exit.

Outside the building, he turned toward the Preparation Facility where Hive workers readied stolen cars and other valuables for shipment to their respective buyers, hoping Agent Grant would be there. Agent 32's hand hurt, his mood was awful, and he'd missed his break time with all of this errand-running. The last thing he wanted to do was go on a scavenger hunt for Agent Grant. As he crossed the courtyard, he paused for a moment and his head snapped to the left.

He stared intently into the darkness. He was almost sure he'd seen movement. He watched a few moments longer but saw nothing further, so he continued toward the Preparation Facility.

He entered and surveyed the commotion inside. Ah yes. Agent Grant stood at the far end of the building talking to a rich-looking Middle Eastern man – probably a potential buyer. Unfortunately this put him in a tough spot: keep the Grand Matron waiting or possibly disrupt a sale. Agent 32 looked at his watch and shuffled uncomfortably trying to decide which was the lesser of the two evils. He opted to just walk briskly toward Agent Grant, trying to look as important as possible, and hope that Agent Grant turned toward him. It worked. About fifteen or so paces away, Agent Grant paused his conversation and turned toward him.

"You look like you're in a hurry for something," asked Agent Grant. "Are you the one who went after the Gunn girl?"

"Yes sir," replied Agent 32. "And the Grand Matron has been informed. She now demands your presence for a little, ah, talk with the girl."

Agent Grant nodded with satisfaction. "Perfect. Thank you. You're dismissed." He then shook hands with the buyer and they parted ways.

Agent 32 walked as quickly as he could from the building hoping to get to the break room before anyone else assigned him further tasks.

***

Agent Grant looked down at his watch and then walked briskly for the exit to meet up with the Grand Matron. About five minutes later, he stood outside

Grand Matron Von Druska's quarters. He knocked and called, "Ma'am, Agent Grant reporting as ordered."

On the other side of the door he heard some shuffling, and then the door opened. The Grand Matron stepped out and smiled at him cruelly. "Ready to do what you do best?" she asked.

"Always," he answered, motioning with his hand that he would follow her lead.

A few turns later, they arrived at the detention wing. Agent Grant stepped forward, swiped his keycard to open the door, and then held it as the Grand Matron walked through. The light was on in the detention wing, but there was no agent standing guard. The Grand Matron looked at him and frowned.

"Where is your guard, Agent Grant?" the Grand Matron asked sternly. "Which agent was assigned detail of the girl?"

"It was originally Agent 32, but I just saw him at the Preparation Facility," replied Agent Grant quickly. "He's the one who informed me you were ready to talk to the Gunn girl. He must've turned her over to another agent – perhaps the one from the gate."

"But then where *is* he?" she asked again.

"I don't kn… ," began Agent Grant, but he quickly changed his answer to, "I'll find out. Maybe he had to visit the bathroom."

The Grand Matron rolled her eyes and said, "Never mind. You can deal with him later. I'm assuming your keycard will open her cell?"

"It does indeed Madam," answered Agent Grant. Now to guess which of the five cells the girl was in. He walked to the first one, swiped his card, and pulled on the handle. It was dark inside – and more importantly empty. He pushed the door closed and walked to the next cell and repeated the previous steps. Again, upon opening the door, he found this cell also dark and vacant. Same thing with the third cell.

He resisted the urge to look over his shoulder at the Grand Matron, but Agent Grant could feel her angry gaze piercing through the back of his head. He moved quickly to the fourth cell, hoping for it to be the right one. It wasn't; it was empty like the three before it.

"I guess it's this last one," muttered Agent Grant as he swiped his card and pulled the handle. To his dismay and surprise, the fifth cell block was as empty as the first four. Now he had no choice but to turn around and face the furious Grand Matron. She did not speak, but her eyes demanded an explanation – something he did not have.

"I apologize Ma'am," Agent Grant began. "There must be some kind of miscommunication. I don't know why she's not here."

Finally the Grand Matron spoke and her voice was full of rage. "Why does it seem that there are so many things that my lead agent doesn't know? Perhaps the task is in the wrong hands."

"Not at all," Agent Grant said quickly, "And I'll call Agent 32 to find out why she's not here. I'm very sorry again."

Agent Grant practically sprinted to the black phone on the wall and called the front gate. No one picked up. Now Agent Grant was getting angry. He hung up and then dialed the barracks. After three rings, the phone picked up, and Agent Grant barked, "Put Agent 32 on, and be quick about it."

After about a minute's wait, the agent on the other end returned and said, "Sorry sir, Agent 32 isn't here. Wasn't he assigned to pick up the Gunn girl? Perhaps he's not back yet."

"He's back," snapped Agent Grant. "I just spoke with him not fifteen minutes ago." Agent Grant slammed the phone down and glanced over at the Grand Matron. All of this was only further angering the Grand Matron. He quickly dialed the break room. The phone picked up and Agent Grant immediately recognized Agent 32's voice on the other end.

"Get down here to the detention wing," Agent Grant ordered.

"Sir I just made a coffee," answered Agent 32 on the other end. "Can it wait until my break is over? I've been on the go for –"

Agent Grant cut him off. "Forget your stupid coffee break! The girl is not in the detention wing – or anywhere to be found."

***

Agent 32 apologized and hung up the phone as he pitched his cup of coffee in the direction of the break room trash can. It missed and burst on the floor but Agent 32 paid it no mind. He quickly strapped on his gun belt, grabbed his hat and ran for the door. Outside he sprinted for the guard station by the front gate. A moment later he arrived and pushed the door open. Empty! He looked over at the gate but it was securely closed.

He ran next to the barracks and slammed into the door sending it flying open. Several agents jumped as the door banged against the wall. "Where's Agent

19?" he demanded loudly. The agents just looked at him and shrugged. "Find him now!" yelled Agent 32. "He had the Gunn girl and they're both missing and the Grand Matron is furious."

An agent sitting at the poker table laughed. "Eh, she's always furious isn't she? Maybe 19 and the girl are having some fun somewhere?" The other agents at the table joined him in laughter.

Agent 32 cursed loudly and began working his way furiously through the barracks, room by room. *Screw those lazy agents,* he thought. "I've been on the go for hours and they can't be bothered to get up and help," he mumbled aloud to himself. He moved from room to room, intentionally making a mess in the other agents' rooms as he searched. "Serves them right for not helping me," he muttered under his breath.

Agent 32 turned into the final room when his watch buzzed again. The screen illuminated bright red with the Hive symbol again. The Grand Matron had grown impatient. He rushed back into the main room to find that everyone else was quickly getting dressed and strapping on their gear. Agent 32 could see that the watches on each of the agents' wrists glowing bright red as well. The Grand Matron must've summoned them all – something Agent 32 couldn't ever remember happening before.

In less than five minutes every Hive agent was assembled in formation outside in the courtyard. There were seventy-five of them in all – or at least there was supposed to be. Though standing at attention, Agent 32 could see out of his peripheral that the spot where Agent 19 should have been standing was conspicuously empty. The compound was illuminated by the flood lights they never used – one of them flickered ominously above where the Grand Matron stood. Agent Grant stood beside her without his usual confident expression on his face.

The Grand Matron broke the silence. "Not once in the history of Hive has a detainee gone missing. That record will not be broken tonight. The prisoner will be found and those responsible for this embarrassment will be punished."

She turned to Agent Grant. "When Agent 19 is found, you will bring him directly to me. Failure will not be tolerated."

Once again she addressed her Hive, "Spread out. Search the compound – every last inch of it if you have to until the girl and our rogue agent are found."

No one immediately moved so Agent Grant shouted almost with a screech, "Go! Now!"

Agents scattered, some in pairs, some in small groups, and others alone, spreading out to cover the compound.

***

Sam and Tiffany were standing in the far right corner of the compound behind the Preparation Building still trying to figure out how the false wall was projected, when suddenly the entire junkyard was illuminated by floodlights. Sam's first instinct was to hit the deck, and he grabbed Tiffany and pulled her to the ground. There was no way this wasn't somehow connected to their presence, though Sam wasn't sure how they'd been discovered. He knew this though, they couldn't just lay there. There was zero cover at this location. He motioned for Tiffany to stand up and follow him. He could see a bit of the front gate, and the coast looked clear.

Sam leaned over to Tiffany. "Our best bet is to make a run for it and get out of here before this place comes alive. Run like you've never run before in your life."

Tiffany nodded and off they ran. But just as they began to sprint forward, the door near the gate burst open and Hive agents began pouring out. Sam skidded to a halt and held out his arm to stop Tiffany. She ran full force into his forearm with her face, knocking her down. As terrible as Sam felt about that, there was no time to waste. He grabbed her roughly by the arm and dragged her to her feet and back the direction they had come. The way to the outside was now impossibly unreachable. The only direction left to run was into the drab world on the other side of the false wall.

Sam and Tiffany sprinted toward it, hoping it wasn't also now swarming with Hive agents.

CHAPTER NINE
GREYTOWN

Sam instinctively flinched as he passed through the false wall and into the concrete world on the other side. Because his eyes were adjusted to the brightness of the floodlights back in the compound, the dreary lighting of the grey world around him seemed even grimmer than before. He was further greeted by the loud whirring of the single-engine private jet that was beginning to taxi down the runway preparing for takeoff – no doubt belonging to the rich businessman he'd seen earlier in the shipping building.

Other than the departing plane, to Sam's relief, the coast seemed clear. He looked around, again taking in the layout of the drab sort of city, trying to determine the best direction to go next. Sam hated to linger too long, but he also hated the thought of running wildly into this unknown territory. With both the helipad and the airstrip now empty, that left just one direction: forward toward the multistory buildings that lay not far ahead. He and Tiffany moved cautiously but rapidly ahead, not knowing if or when they'd be swarmed by Hive agents.

As they neared the first building Tiffany whispered, "Should we see what's inside?"

Sam nodded and unholstered his service weapon. He looked for a doorknob to open the door, but there wasn't one. Not like it had been removed; the door just didn't have one. It was then he noticed the small black square panel about shoulder height on the door. Sam ran his fingers over it looking for a button or something, but it was smooth and lacking anything of the kind. Sam pushed on it with his palm. Still nothing happened. Then he remembered the keypad at the first building. He fished the keycard out of his shirt pocket and held it next to the black panel.

With a whoosh that made him jump back and made Tiffany stifle a shriek, the door retracted up at an alarming speed into the door frame above it. It reminded Sam of something he'd seen in a space movie. As Sam tried to peer into the darkness inside, suddenly with equally blinding speed, the door returned from the slot above it and shut tightly.

Sam couldn't help letting out a gasp. "Ooh boy," he said half to himself. "That's quite a door. Liable to take a man's hand off if he's not careful."

"I know, right? Wonder where they get doors like that," answered Tiffany with a shudder. She took a firmer grip on the rifle she was carrying and then asked, "Should we go in?"

Sam frowned as he pondered his answer. "It's awful dark inside. I don't know what we'd be walking into. I'd like to take a look at the other buildings, but I suspect they're all like this one. I just wish I knew what we might find inside. Hey what did you do with that flashlight I handed you from the guard back at the gate?"

Tiffany patted her pockets and found it in the agent's jacket she'd taken. Sam took it and switched it on. He then raised the keycard up to the panel again.

Like before it quickly snapped up and open. Tiffany started to take a step forward to go inside, but Sam put his arm across her path and whispered, "I want to count how long it takes for the door to close again. That's the kind of door you don't want to get caught in."

The door whooshed shut. Sam nodded for Tiffany to scan the keycard again, and as soon as the door opened Sam began counting under his breath. "One, two, three, four, five, six –" At the count of six, the door slid shut again. "Six seconds doesn't sound like a lot of time, but should be plenty of time to go in and out. Scan it again, and we'll go."

Tiffany scanned the keypad again, and in they went. Sam scanned the room with the beam of the flashlight. It was so dark, that the flashlight did little more than cast wild shadows. They stood there for a moment, waiting for their eyes to adjust to the dimness. Sam scanned the walls of the room looking for a light switch. On the wall, there was a dome-shaped light, but neither Sam nor Tiffany could find a switch.

Tiffany walked over to the light and felt around it with her hand. As soon as her hand touched the globe, it came on. "Hey that's cool," said Tiffany. "It's one of those touch lights."

It wasn't a very bright light, but it did allow Sam to put the flashlight away. There wasn't much to the room. Really it wasn't much more than a foyer. To the left and to the right was each a room, and in front of them, separated by a section of wall, were two hallways.

"I suppose we should check out these doors first," whispered Sam. He chose the door on the right first. "Watch my back while I check out this one. If anything comes out, shoot 'em – and I'm serious."

Sam reached for the door. No fancy keypad on this one; just a regular doorknob. It turned easily. The light in the room came on automatically which, as on-edge as Sam was, made him jump. He held his service pistol up at ready as he peeked quickly inside the room. It was empty except for a long table with chairs.

"What's in there," asked Tiffany in a low voice.

"Nothing really," Sam responded. "Looks like a boardroom of some kind."

Tiffany, walking backwards so that her front remained toward the room she was supposed to cover and then looking over her shoulder, glanced into the room. "I'd say it was a dining room," she said.

Sam nodded. "Actually, I think you're right. It's empty though and there's no doors leading off of it, so I might as well check out the other one." He quietly closed the door, and as it latched, the light inside automatically shut off. Sam walked quietly across the foyer and, reaching down to the knob, opened the door on the left. This time no light came on. Still Sam was sort of able to see inside the room thanks to the light spillover from the foyer.

Inside the room were three adult-sized bunk beds. There wasn't enough light for Sam to confirm if they were occupied or not. However he suspected they were because on the ground neatly folded on the floor next to each bed was two piles of the same kind of drab gray jump suits he'd seen early on the workers in the shipping facility. He stared motionless, allowing his eyes to further adjust to the dimness of the room. By now he was convinced that all six beds were occupied. He looked at his watch. It was now nearly two a.m.

Behind him, Tiffany began to ask what was in there, but he quickly held up his hand to silence her. Sam honestly didn't know what they should do. Even if these were some of the Missing, Sam wasn't sure that waking them was the right course of action – but he also didn't like the idea of exploring the rest of the building knowing that there were six unidentified people that could wake up at any moment. After a moment longer, Sam opted to just leave the room.

"What is it?" Tiffany asked. "What did you see? What was in there?"

"It was a dormitory of some sort, I think."

"Was it empty?"

"Nope. I'm pretty sure there were six people sleeping in there."

Tiffany sucked in her breath and clapped a hand over her mouth. "What are we going to do?"

After a moment of silence, Sam answered, "I don't know. Part of me says to leave you here to guard the door, but I don't like the idea of us splitting up. But I also don't like the idea of us going off together, knowing that they could wake up at any moment and corner us somewhere. I'm also tempted to just exit the building and search something else."

"Well, if you want my vote, I say we search the rest of the building ," said Tiffany. "I don't like not knowing what's in here."

Sam considered a moment longer and then agreed. "Ok let's take the right hallway."

As they walked, motion activated LED lights illuminated along the baseboard. There was nothing noteworthy to see in the hallway until they reached the end where they encountered a staircase heading up. So up they went. At the top was a wide hallway with doors lining each side.

"Probably more dorms if I had to guess," said Sam. He quickly counted the doors. Four on each side for a total of eight. "Geez!" he exclaimed under his breath. Tiffany looked at him quizzically. "I just did the math," Sam whispered. "If each of these rooms has six beds, and all of them are full, then we're talking about eight times six…forty-eight people. And then you add in the six more downstairs, and we've potentially got fifty-four people in this building. And if the rest of the matching buildings outside – what were there, like nine or ten more – if they're like this one, we're talking hundreds of people."

"Only one way to find out," said Tiffany as she moved to the first door on the left. Sam quickly intercepted her hand before she reached the door handle and gestured that he would take the lead. Tiffany tried to peer inside but again Sam motioned for her to watch the hallway and the stairway they'd just come up.

Inside the room, it was a little harder to see this time without the spillover light from the foyer downstairs, but Sam's eyes were by now mostly adjusted to the dark. It was as he feared, but worse. This room had four sets of bunk beds, not three. And at the foot of each bed lay two piles of neatly folded clothes. And he could see the lump of a human form in each bed.

Sam ducked back out and silently closed the door. "It's just like the room downstairs," he whispered to Tiffany, "except eight occupied beds instead of six.

Which means if I've under-calculated the total number of people in here by at least ten or twelve. Let's check the rest real fast to be sure."

As Sam suspected, each of the other seven rooms upstairs were identical to the first: eight beds; eight people per room. The hallway ended at a bathroom on the right and another staircase going up on the left.

"Wait," Tiffany exclaimed. "Didn't you say these buildings were like at least six stories tall? If the next five stories are just like this one, then your math was actually super low. There'd be like, what –" She counted quickly in her head. "Like three hundred people in just this building? So total in all the apartments, if they're all full, that'd be thousands, not hundreds."

"I think you're right," Sam said. "And I hate that you're right. But you most definitely are." Sam rubbed his tired eyes. "You know, when I made this plan earlier this evening I was not prepared to deal with thousands of people. I don't know exactly what I was expecting but it wasn't all this."

They climbed the next set of stairs with Tiffany glancing occasionally over her shoulder behind them. The third floor was identical to the one below them: four doors on the left; four on the right; a bathroom at the end of the hall on the right and another staircase going up. It took Sam about five minutes to check each room, and as best as he could tell, they were occupied the same as the floor below: eight beds per room; sixty-four occupants in total.

As they arrived back at the staircase, Sam pointed for them to head up to the next level. "I'm gonna get my leg work out today with all these stairs," joked Tiffany. Sam smiled. It was nice to smile. It had been way too long.

The fourth floor was a surprise to Sam. It appeared to be a mirror image of the first floor rather than the previous two floors beneath them. To the left and to the right was only a single door each. Sam checked the door on the left, and, as expected it held three bunk beds, all occupied. Sam opened the door on the right and as just like on the first floor, it was another dining room. And like the one on the first floor, the light came on automatically as the door opened.

Sam was just about to shut the door, when he noticed a line on the far wall that ran from floor to ceiling. Sam whispered for Tiffany to stand watch in the hallway as he investigated further. Sam was now sure that the line on the wall was the door to an elevator. And sure enough, there was a button on the right just like you'd expected for an elevator.

He hurried back to Tiffany and said in a hushed voice, "There's an elevator on the back wall. There was probably one in the first floor dining room too. I must've missed it."

"Can we please take it?" asked Tiffany. "I mean, my legs probably need the workout and all, but it'd be faster and easier."

Sam thought for a moment. "I don't think that'll work. If I'm correct, there should be just one more floor above us. And if I had to guess, I'd say that the elevator most likely only goes down from here, back to the first floor since we haven't seen any elevators on any of the other dorm room floors."

"Well then after we check the top floor, can we come back down here and ride it back down?" asked Tiffany hopefully.

"We'll see," replied Sam.

Tiffany rolled her eyes. "You sound like my dad."

Sam smiled and shrugged. "Gotta practice for when my boys grow up." Sam closed his eyes and silently prayed that they'd get out of there alive and he'd get that chance.

Sam closed the dining room door and the light went off. Once again, he pointed up the stairs. "Last set of stairs hopefully."

Indeed the top floor was as Sam guessed: four doors on each side; no stairs and no elevator; just a mostly-empty storage room at the end of the hall where stairs would have been. Sam cleared each room as quickly as he could, and about three minutes later, reported to Tiffany, "All beds full. I guess down we go."

Tiffany led the way down. On the fourth floor she stopped in the middle of the hallway. Sam whispered, "What's the matter?"

Tiffany looked back at him with puppy dog eyes. "That elevator sounds awful nice," she said and let her voice trail off.

Sam made a face that reflected mild annoyance. "We'll check it out. No promises." He opened the dining room door again and was once again blinded by the light coming on automatically. "There goes my night vision…again."

They made their way to the elevator on the far wall, and Tiffany reached out eagerly and pushed the button. The doors opened silently, and they walked into the elevator. There were just two buttons on the panel inside: one marked "D1" and the other marked with only the letter "B."

Sam pressed the one labeled "D1" and as they rode down he said out loud more to himself than to Tiffany, "I'm guessing 'B' stands for basement. I kinda forgot about the other hallway on the first floor. My guess is that it has a staircase going to an underground basement."

"Wonder what's down there," Tiffany replied. "My guess is a kitchen. They have two dining rooms and they've gotta feed all these people."

Sam looked at Tiffany and smiled. "I like how normal and practical you think. I was imagining a guard station and other dangerous stuff like that, but you're probably right."

The elevator slowed, indicating they were arriving at their destination. As the doors opened, Sam readied his pistol just in case. However it opened as they expected into the empty dining room, presumably on the first floor. As they stepped out of the elevator, the light flicked on. Cautiously Sam opened the dining room door. The light from the dining room cast creepy shadows into the foyer. Sam peered carefully around the room, but it was empty just like they'd left it. The dome light Tiffany had first turned on was no longer illuminated. While Sam held the door to light the foyer, he whispered to Tiffany to go activate the foyer light again.

As soon as it was on, he closed the dining room door. Sam stood there for a minute waiting for his eyes to adjust to the dimness of the foyer. He checked his watch again: 3:12AM. It had taken them a lot longer to clear the building than he had originally counted on. He guessed they had just about two and a half hours of darkness remaining before sunrise. Sam didn't like the thought of what sunrise might bring as this place came to life.

As Sam began to move, Tiffany headed straight for the hallway on the left. Sam whispered for her to hold. "Hang on, I want to just check this first room again, and make sure everyone is in their bed like we left them." He opened the door and scanned the room. His night vision wasn't back full yet, but with the little bit of light shining in the room from the foyer, it looked like everyone was in their place. Satisfied, Sam shut the door again without a sound.

"Ok let's check out the other hallway and I'm assuming the basement below," he whispered to Tiffany. Like before, the hallway gradually illuminated more and more as sets of LED's switched on before their feet. Halfway down the hallway, Sam could see the stairway at the end, but on the right was another door. Sam was about to reach for the handle when he noticed that light was coming from underneath it. Since all the lighting in the building seemed to be on a timer, that meant that most likely someone was in the room.

CHAPTER TEN
GESTAPO

After a thorough search of the compound, Agent Grant returned to the Grand Matron. "Yes?" she asked impatiently. "Have you found her?"

Agent Grant swallowed and hesitated. "No, Madam. She is definitely not in the compound. We've searched every last inch of it."

The Grand Matron's face turned a deep red with anger and her hand moved to the pistol at her waist. Agent Grant's eyes grew wide with terror and he quickly spoke, choosing his words carefully, knowing his life very well depended on what he said next. "I think she had help. You know the missing agent – Agent 19 we were looking for? Well, we found him. He was unconscious and zip tied in a ditch just outside the gate. He had a large bump on the back of his head. There's no way the Gunn girl overpowered our agent. Plus she was handcuffed when she was picked up. Someone must've helped her get free."

That news did nothing to abate the Grand Matron's mood. "Do we have a defector then? What about Agent 32, the one who originally retrieved the girl?"

"I tentatively locked him up in the holding cells," answered Agent Grant, "but I questioned him quite harshly and I'm convinced he had no part in her disappearance."

"*You're* convinced," the Grand Matron seethed sarcastically. "Oh. Well, then I suppose that clears up everything."

"Madam, I'm sure of it actually. He told me he handed the girl off to Agent 19 and then reported straight to you. We checked the timestamps both at the gate keypad and at the keycard panel on the bunker. There's only four minutes between them. There simply wouldn't have been enough time for him to do anything with her and still report to you as quickly as he did."

"So, who then?"

"If I had to wager a guess I'd say it is Detective Cross. But I'm not sure how. Our agents have been watching the old woman's place and his bedroom door hasn't opened and his car is still there."

The Grand matron cursed. "So you're telling me we've been wasting our time searching the compound? They'd be foolish to remain here. They must've escaped back into town."

"That would be my guess, too, Madam."

"I want you to mobilize every agent and send them door to door. Search the park, every restaurant, drag shopkeepers out of their homes and make them open their stores. If they refuse, break their doors down. Leave a barebones crew here to guard the compound and to deal with the workers when they wake up. But the rest are to search the town. I don't want to see your face again until they're found!"

Agent Grant didn't wait to be dismissed. He was just happy to see the Grand Matron's hand leave her sidearm.

Soon he and sixty fellow agents were racing out of the compound in their black SUVs. They fanned out across the town waking the townsfolk despite it being not even 3:00AM yet. At each house, groups of four agents would bang on the door and once the homeowner answered, without even explaining their purpose, three of the Hive agents would force their way inside and begin tossing the house room by room. The fourth agent would then question the frightened residents.

Agent Grant expected their search to go well into the morning. Hamlin had exactly 1255 homes – in addition to the shops, the lake park, plus the school that would all have to be searched. And with just fifteen teams of four agents, it would be a grueling process.

In fact, he reckoned they'd be lucky to be done before lunch. Speaking of lunch, Agent Grant couldn't remember the last time he had eaten. His empty stomach only further soured an already bad mood.

Agent Grant headed with his team toward Mrs. Gena's. He didn't like the old woman and he was looking forward to harassing her and personally messing up her tidy little place. At Gena's he sent one agent to guard the side door that led to Detective Cross's room, while he and the other two agents approached the front door. The two agents in the SUV across the street that had been watching the exit joined him.

At the door, Agent Grant began banging on it with his gloved fist. Moments later a light came on and he heard Mrs. Gena's frail voice saying, "I'm coming! I'm coming! Is that you Sam?" Agent Grant kept pounding.

He could hear Mrs. Gena fumbling with the lock, and as soon as the door opened a crack, he shoved it in and forced his way inside. Gena fell *hard* to the ground. Agent Grant stepped over her, cursing. “Get up!” When she was slow to rise, he yelled and cursed at her again.

Trembling and holding onto the wall for support, Mrs. Gena painfully pulled herself to her feet. “W-what’s the matter?” she stammered. “How can I help you gentlemen? Would you like some fresh cookies from supper?”

Agent Grant sent the four agents that were with him to search the house. It made him even angrier that he hadn’t been able to dampen her cheery and polite demeanor. “Does it look like I came for a social visit?” replied Agent Grant with venom in his voice. “Where’s that detective? And where’s the Gunn girl?”

“Oh, Sam and Tiffany?” replied Mrs. Gena. “I’ve not seen Tiffany since –” She winced painfully before finishing her sentence. “Since she came over this afternoon to play the piano for a bit.”

“And the Detective?” asked Agent Grant.

“Not seen him since a little after dinner,” answered Mrs. Gena with a straight face. “I think he went to the store early in the evening but he went in and out of his own door, I reckon. I had a headache and so I went to bed early.”

“I could care less about your health,” spat Agent Grant. “You and your Pollyanna look on life makes me sick. And if I find out you’re lying to me about anything, you can take a little ride with me and join the rest of those who resist Hive.”

"Such poor, nice folks," muttered Mrs. Gena at the mention of the Missing.

A few minutes later, the agents returned. "Place is empty, except for her."

Agent Grant turned angrily to Mrs. Gena. "I thought you said Detective Cross was in his room. Why is it empty then? Where did he go? Stop lying to me you old bat!" Agent Grant raised his hand as though he'd hit her.

Mrs. Gena's eyes flashed back and she stood her ground. "I said what I said. And you can holler and use that filthy language and even break every bone in my body, but it's not gonna change my answer. He came to supper. I heard him go out a little while later. And then I heard him come back. If he's not in his room, then I don't have the foggiest idea where he's gone to. You have your watchers everywhere, I suggest you ask *them* how he slipped past."

Agent Grant was taken back and slightly amused by the old woman's spunk. "I didn't think you had it in you," he said with a half grin. "Alright boys," he said to the agents. "Let's go. You four come with me. And I'll leave Agent 53 here to sit with the woman just in case." And with that he stormed out the door.

Mrs. Gena collapsed into the chair by the fireplace and placed a hand on her chest. She'd never been so scared in her whole life, yet never so bold either. All those years earlier when they'd forced her to stay, she hadn't stood up for herself. But she was glad that she did this time.

Her hip and shoulder ached from being knocked down by Agent Grant, so she decided to just see if she could doze off right here in the big comfy chair. She closed her eyes and began to pray for Sam.

***

By midmorning most of the town had been searched, with the exception of the park and school grounds. Agent Grant had saved them for last, knowing it'd go much faster with all the agents converging together. Once they were all gathered at the park, Agent Grant took a report.

"Anyone give you any trouble? Anyone I need to go back and visit – or maybe pick up?" Agent Grant asked.

Most of the Hive teams reported little to no resistance except the team led by Agent 73. "Might need to visit the Jackson residence. I thought for sure they were hiding something the way they argued and blocked the door. But turns out they just thought they had a choice in the matter."

Agent Grant made a note in his notepad. "Anyone else?"

"Sheriff Gunn," said Agent 44. "He was still out from that shot Agent 32 gave him, but he woke up while I was back in his daughter's room."

"The Sheriff definitely needs a visit," replied Agent Grant, making a note.

"Yeah, he acted like we were allies or something. Kept trying to get information out of us, but I told him to shut up. Actually thought I was going to have to restrain him there for a minute though. But I threatened to take him to the Grand Matron and that got him back in line."

"Good, good," said Agent Grant. "Anything else."

"Just that he got mad again when I told him to stay inside. But for all his fussing, he finally did what he always does – exactly what he's told."

Agent Grant laughed. "A useful idiot for sure. Alright, if that's it, then let's fan out and search the lake area. Be thorough now. Check the tall grasses, the trees – everything. I want to catch these troublemakers and get back to business as usual."

CHAPTER ELEVEN
AWAKE

Sam readied his gun and reached for the doorknob when he heard the flush of a toilet from the other side. Figuring surprise was on their side, he quickly pulled Tiffany to where they'd be behind the door when it opened. Agonizing seconds ticked by and finally the door opened. Sam aimed his gun, finger just off the trigger, ready to fire if need be. Out walked a woman. She was dressed only in drab grey underwear. She closed the bathroom door behind her. Sam and Tiffany stood like statues, hoping they wouldn't be seen.

So far so good. The woman walked down the hallway, her back toward them, in the direction of the foyer. However, as she turned toward the dorm room off the foyer and reached for the doorknob, she hesitated a moment. Her head slowly turned toward Sam and Tiffany. She stared at them for what was probably no longer than a second but seemed like an eternity, and then continued inside the dorm room and closed the door silently behind her.

"What was that?" asked Tiffany.

"Weird is what that was," answered Sam, "And bad. We've been discovered."

"She didn't seem to care though," Tiffany replied. "And why was she in her underwear? And I thought you said everybody was in their beds when you checked a minute ago?"

"Evidently I missed someone," Sam said annoyed. "It was dark, and as you just saw, her clothes were still beside the bed on the ground. Six piles of clothes. Should've meant six people in bed."

"More importantly," Sam continued, "is what we should do next. She definitely saw us. I just don't know what to do about it."

"This isn't a spy movie," retorted Tiffany. "We can't just off her."

Sam snorted a laugh. "That's definitely not what I meant. I'm just honestly confused by her reaction to seeing us. She didn't seem to really care."

"Maybe she thought we were Hive agents?" suggested Tiffany. "I am wearing one of their jackets – though I've never seen a woman Hive agent. It could be though that in the dark she didn't even realize I was a girl."

"Yeah maybe," said Sam.

"Also, did you see her eyes? I mean the way she looked at us. I only saw her eyes for a second, but they seemed…I don't know what the word for it is."

Sam finished her thought, "Vacant. Empty."

"Exactly," exclaimed Tiffany trying to keep her voice down. "It reminded me of some of the people in the pictures from the records room."

"You're absolutely right," said Sam. "There was something almost robotic about the way she came out of the bathroom and walked back to her room. Even when she looked at us, it wasn't normal."

Tiffany suddenly had a thought. She squeezed Sam's arm tightly as she spoke, "If she was one of the

Missing, does that mean everyone in this building and maybe the rest of buildings here aren't Hive at all?"

"`Did you recognize her?" asked Sam.

"No, but still, who else would they be?" answered Tiffany.

"There's a good chance you're right," Sam said thoughtfully. "And there's that airstrip and helipad outside. I suppose it's possible that some of these people aren't even from Hamlin, but brought in from somewhere else. But even if they're the Missing, that doesn't explain her eyes and behavior. I wonder if they could be brainwashed or something."

Tiffany shrugged. "It *was* weird, or maybe, like I said, she just thought we were Hive."

Sam looked at his watch: 3:25AM. "We've been standing here long enough," he said. "If that woman was coming back out, she would've done so by now. Let's continue down the hallway."

As they suspected, at the end of the hallway was a set of stairs headed down. Sam instructed Tiffany to crouch on the stairs and watch the foyer behind them until he gave the signal for her to continue downstairs. Tiffany nodded and Sam cautiously descended.

The red LEDs on the stairs cast eerie shadows that played tricks with his mind making him imagine he kept seeing movement. The basement was similar in design as the ground floor above him: an open space and a door to the left and the right. Across the room in front of him were two doors marked "Utility." Sam checked these first just to confirm, and sure enough, one was a large closet with cleaning supplies and the other contained the furnace, breaker panel, and a tool bench. Sam poked through the drawers on the workbench, deciding to grab a pair of needle nose pliers and a screwdriver. He put them in his cargo pants – *Just in case,* he thought.

Back now in the hallway he was facing the stairs again. He decided to first check the door that was now on his right. Instead of a doorknob, it had a pull handle. He slowly pulled it open. It was a storage room. Inside were all kinds of food and cooking supplies: bags and bags of flour; bottles of oil; large bags of rice and beans – simple yet filling food staples. A large fridge contained what you'd expect: a dozen gallons of milk, cartons of eggs, lots of butter, cheese, and various fruits and vegetables. There were also several vials of a clear liquid. Sam wasn't sure what to make of them, but he was suddenly hungry. He grabbed a block of cheese and two small apples and put them in his pocket for him and Tiffany to share. Nothing else caught his eye other than a couple bottles of water which he also took, so he exited the room.

He walked quickly across the hallway to the door on the opposite side. Again, the handle was a pull-style one rather than a knob. He opened it and looked around. It was an industrial kitchen: large stoves, fryers, multiple ovens – exactly what you'd need to feed sixty plus people three times a day. And as expected, on the opposite wall was the basement elevator. There wasn't much for Sam to see, so he exited the room and began climbing the stairs.

"Finally," whispered Tiffany impatiently when she saw him. "What's down there?"

"Sorry," Sam whispered back as he glanced at his watch. Somehow he'd been down there for half an hour. It was now almost 4:00AM. "There were a couple utility rooms, a huge food pantry, and a big kitchen like what you'd expect to see in a restaurant; and the elevator.

"Did you say 'food pantry'?" asked Tiffany. "I'm *starving*." She made sure to emphasize that last word.

"How about an apple?" said Sam as he produced one from his pocket.

"It's a start," she answered.

"I have cheese too," Sam said with a smile.

"My hero," joked Tiffany. "I guess right here's not the best place to eat a snack though. And I don't know what I'd do with the apple core. But at least I know we have food. I could use a drink though. I'm parched."

"I have just the thing," answered Sam, pulling a bottle of water from another cargo pocket.

Tiffany unscrewed the lid and downed the entire bottle in one long chug. She wiped at a little water that had escaped her mouth onto her chin and noticed Sam looking at her with slight amazement. "Did I mention I was thirsty," she laughed.

"As long as you don't have to pee later at some inopportune time," Sam whispered back. "I learned doing stakeouts with the police force that it's sometimes best to only sip water as needed and stay in a state of mild dehydration to prevent nature's call."

"Oof," answered Tiffany. "And my dad always tells me I have 'TB' – Tiny Bladder syndrome. I guess we'll find out."

"We'd better get going," Sam said as he glanced again at his watch. "We don't have a lot of darkness left. I can't think of any reason to stay here, though I'm still worried some about that woman who saw us. Did you see any movement at all while you were up here waiting for me?"

"Nothing. Nada. Zilch," Tiffany answered.

"Okay, let's go," said Sam as he headed back down the hallway toward the foyer. Sam glanced at the bottom of the bathroom door just to make sure the light was off and it was. The small dome light in the foyer had also shut itself off again by this time, but Sam left it off since they were exiting the building.

A tiny red light above the front door indicated the sensor that would open the door with blinding speed. Sam and Tiffany approached it and as it whooshed opened, Sam surveyed the outdoors. He counted in his head as he checked the situation outside. Six seconds later, the door whooshed shut. Sam hadn't seen anything outside of concern. It was still dark and to his surprise and relief, there were no signs of any of Hive's agents.

Sam whispered, "Let's go," and raised his hand to wave at the sensor. The door whisked open again and he and Tiffany darted through. A couple seconds later, it closed behind them.

"Where to now?" asked Tiffany.

Sam didn't answer right away as he considered their options. Finally he said, "Let's go around the backside of the next building and eat a snack. I'd like to just take a glance inside each of the buildings to confirm they're more of the same. I don't think we need to check them room by room again, but I'd like to just be sure they're not different types of buildings. But no reason to do it hungry."

Sam and Tiffany sat on the hard-packed earth behind the second building and cracked into the food.

Tiffany took a bite of her apple. "I just realized I haven't eaten since dinner last night – you know because of the whole kidnapping thing." She wiped a dribble of juice that escaped from her lips down her chin. "Sorry. I normally have better manners than this. I'm just so hungry."

Sam waved her off, "No judgment here from me."

Once her apple was gone, she said, "How about that cheese?"

"Sure," said Sam, "And if the rest of these are like the building we just left, then they should all have a pantry, and we can grab another block."

The block of cheese was small, maybe ten ounces. Since Tiffany seemed so hungry, Sam broke off a larger portion for her. She smiled and thanked him, and then began chomping her way through it like she had the apple. A couple minutes later, they were done.

Tiffany held up her apple core. "What do I do with this? I don't see a trash can."

She started to chunk it away, but Sam stopped her. "We don't want to leave evidence of our presence. Either eat it, or pocket it."

Tiffany gave a disgusted look. "Ew. Please tell me you didn't eat the core."

"Nope," said Sam and patted his pocket.

Tiffany grimaced and stuck the wet, sticky apple core in her jacket pocket.

Sam stood up and Tiffany followed suit, and they walked toward the front side of the building. At the door, Tiffany, like before, swiped her access card. And just like the door at the previous building, this one opened with blinding speed. Just to be sure the timing was the same, Sam counted until it closed. Exactly six seconds later it whooshed shut. He nodded for Tiffany to swipe again, and in they went.

As Sam suspected, this building appeared to be just like the last one: a foyer with a door to the right, another to the left, and two long hallways straight ahead. Tiffany walked over and touched the dome light and it came on. "Should we split up to check it faster? I mean, not on separate floors, but I can check the dining room and you can check the bedroom."

"Sure," answered Sam.

"Oh," said Tiffany with a tone of sarcasm, "and actually make sure everyone is in their bed."

"Yeah, yeah," replied Sam.

Sam headed left and Tiffany headed right. Tiffany opened her door and as the light flipped on, she scanned the room: empty like in the last building except for the dining room table. And like before, an elevator in the far wall. She crossed the room and pushed the button to open the doors. It was empty. She waited for the doors to close and then crossed the room and exited. Sam was just closing the door to the dorm room as she came back out. He gave her the "what's up" head gesture.

"Nothing," she replied. "Empty. Same as like the last building. What about you?"

"Six beds, all full," Sam answered.

"You sure?" asked Tiffany with a wink.

"Yesss," Sam said as he rolled his eyes. "And let's just real quick check the other floors. I want to see if the layout is the same."

"Ugh, not more stairs," Tiffany moaned.

Sam smiled. "Yep, but I promise we can ride the elevator back down."

"Deal," said Tiffany.

Up they went. They stopped on each floor, not checking the individual rooms, but just to see if the layout was the same. At the top floor, both Sam and Tiffany were winded and puffing from climbing all the stairs.

"You know, this rifle is heavier than it looks," Tiffany said through ragged breathing as she leaned it against the wall.

"Wanna take a quick rest before going down to the fourth floor and catching the elevator to the bottom?" Sam panted.

"I could actually use another bottle of water," said Tiffany, picking up her rifle. "Let's just get down to the pantry in the basement, assuming it's there like it should be, and then we can rest with water – and maybe another apple."

A minute or so later, they were in the elevator and Tiffany pushed the "B" button for the basement. The doors opened to the empty hallway below. Sam took a quick peek inside both the utility rooms, gave Tiffany a "thumbs up" for all clear. Sam also looked quickly in the kitchen. It too was empty.

"Now for that bottled water and a moment's rest," Tiffany said cheerfully as she reached for the handle to the pantry. Inside it was stocked eerily similar – like identical to how the storage room in the first building was stocked. He grabbed a couple bottles of water for now and a couple for later, handed one to Tiffany and headed for a stack of bean sacks to sit on. Tiffany settled on a stack of rice bags.

"Why do I have to be so scrawny," Tiffany moaned. "If I was just a little fluffier, I could probably nap right here. Ah, sleep. I think I could sleep an entire day after being kidnapped and climbing all those stairs."

She stood up to rearrange her stack of rice sacks, but Sam cautioned against it. "This place is *way* too OCD. I have a feeling they'll notice if something is out of place."

"Well are your beans any more comfy than these rice sacks?"

"Yeah, they're not bad. Trade?"

"Sure, I appreciate it."

"We'll take a quick breather, and then move to the next building."

"Ugh, what were there – like eight more?" Tiffany grumbled.

"Something like that. We'll just take it one at a time."

"After my legs have a rest, please. And I'm gonna have buns of steel after all those stairs."

They sat in silence sipping their water. They had been sitting so still that after five minutes the motion sensor turned the light off. Sam groaned that he had to get up and reactivate the light, but Tiffany begged him not to.

"The dark feels nice. Let's leave it that way," she said.

Sam glanced at his watch: 4:40AM. "Ok, fifteen minutes max, and we gotta go."

***

The light suddenly flicked on and Sam started to his feet. *Son of a gun,* he thought as panic spread over him. *We must've fallen asleep.* He reached over to Tiffany who was still sound asleep, and swatted her leg to awaken her.

Sam rubbed his eyes and looked at his watch. "Shoot," he exclaimed. "It's 6:00AM. We were only supposed to rest fifteen minutes, not an hour and a half. It's probably light outside now. Getting out of here is going to be much trickier."

Tiffany yawned and grabbed her rifle. "I guess let's go then," she said with another yawn. Her backside was stiff from her makeshift bed. "Also," she added, "I need to visit the bathroom. Was there one on this floor?"

"We need to be super careful. There could be people awake now. I don't know what caused the light to come on." Sam cautioned.

"Oh you didn't activate it by waking up?" Tiffany asked.

"Nope, it just came on," Sam said worried. "It's what woke me up. And the fact that it came on exactly at six makes me think it was on a timer – which probably means every other light in the building is set the same way. I'm really worried that there is fixing to be a lot of activity in this place."

Sam unholstered his handgun and crept toward the door. Mentally he was beating himself up for allowing this to happen. As he reached for the door, he heard a noise outside and the door swung inward. Sam and Tiffany jumped back and flattened themselves against the wall wishing for some kind of cover. There was none. Sam readied his baton with his left hand and his gun in this right.

In walked four women dressed in their drab jumpsuits. For the moment they seemed intent on the fridge directly in front of them and the stacks of flour to the left. Sam held his breath. As soon as all their backs were turned to them, he and Tiffany dashed out the door. And ran smack into another one – a man this time, dressed in the same drab jumpsuit. He looked at first startled but then a demented snarl came over his face.

Sam didn't wait to see what he might do and with one swift motion, his baton came across the left temple of the man and he crumpled to the ground. Tiffany stood in shocked horror. She was finally jarred out of her stupor by Sam urging, "Come on! Help me drag him into the utility room. We can hide him behind the workbench."

Tiffany slung her rifle over her back and grabbed the man's feet. He was tall, about six foot four inches and so she could do little more than barely lift him off the ground. A couple minutes later however, the man had been searched by Sam and zip tied to the workbench out of sight.

"This is bad, very bad," Sam complained as he slowly pushed the door open a crack and glanced back into the hallway. Just as Sam was about to exit the room, he heard a voice yell down the stairs, "Where's S71? Why isn't the table set yet? Moronic giant of an oaf!"

Sam looked back at Tiffany. Her eyes were wide with fear. A moment later, a Hive agent arrived at the bottom of the steps. "Must've missed his serum dose somehow and wandered off," the agent grumbled. He opened the door to the kitchen and yelled inside, "One of you slugs get the table set on F1. Let's go! Busy day of work ahead for you. Big shipment going out next week. Let's go, let's go!"

A woman rushed out and headed across the hall toward the pantry. The agent grabbed her for a moment and kissed her and groped her as she attempted to pass by him. She stood passively until he released her a moment later, and then rushed on her way into the pantry.

Sam was disgusted and angered by what he just witnessed. It took a great deal of willpower not to rush out and attack the guard. A moment later, the woman who had been assaulted by the agent hurried back out of the storage room carrying a stack of plates and into the kitchen headed for the elevator.

Despite a strong urge to charge the agent, Sam watched and waited. The agent looked down at his watch and then stuck his head back in the kitchen one last time and yelled, "Hurry it up!" before heading back upstairs.

CHAPTER TWELVE
CONTROL

"What just happened," whispered Tiffany. "And what was it he said about a serum?"

"I think I might be beginning to understand the empty look in the eyes of that woman we saw earlier this morning," Sam explained. "I think Hive keeps the Missing drugged 24/7. That explains the behavior of the woman in the bathroom this morning, the way those four ladies just walked passed us in the pantry, and even the way the man tied up behind us acted. And what you didn't see a moment ago was an agent kissing and groping a woman and she didn't even flinch. The serum must be a hypnotic, mind-control something or other."

"You realize how crazy that sounds when you say it out loud," Tiffany said, "And yet with the history of this town and all we've seen, it also sounds like the most logical explanation."

Just then Sam remembered the vials of clear liquid he had seen in the fridge. "I think I've actually seen the serum. They keep it in the fridge in these little vials like you'd see in a lab. My guess is that they mix it with the food."

"Wait, wait, wait," Tiffany whispered excitedly. "I'm having a brainstorm. The Hive agent made it sound like if they miss their serum dose, the effects begin to wear off after about a day. But maybe not entirely off for another day after that."

"Yeah?" Sam said.

"Ok, well, what if we just go into the kitchens of all the buildings and take all the serum – pour it down the drain, smash it – whatever. If they miss a day of serum, they'll stop doing their work, and after another day they will hopefully be back to normal. And then we can rally them all against Hive for a revolt and free the town! What do you think?"

Sam stroked his chin. "*If* we could pull it off, which is a big if since I'm sure all the buildings are awake right now, it would certainly cause some mayhem. But it would also alert Hive to our presence, and it seems like, at least so far, they don't have a clue we're here. I think we should keep it that way. Plus, I'm fairly positive they manufacture the stuff here somewhere, so they likely would just go get more. It's a decent idea, but probably wouldn't ultimately work."

Tiffany's shoulders slumped. "Ok, well what's your plan then?"

"To be honest, I don't have one yet," Sam admitted. "But just because we don't have a good plan, doesn't mean we need to rush headlong into a bad one – no offense."

Tiffany nodded.

Sam continued, "I think we should hide out here for a little while, since we're in a safe spot. That agent mentioned something about everyone going to work on some kind of shipment, and so I'm guessing then we'll be able to sneak out. After that, I honestly am not sure what our best play is."

"Well, so far we've been winging it pretty good; why start planning now," Tiffany said with a laugh.

***

Time seemed to creep by as they waited for the Missing to finish up their breakfast chores. Tiffany traded spots with Sam so she could watch the occasional person walk by. The near mindless way they walked and carried out their tasks, really shook her. Thoughts of her friend Laura – and maybe her mother also, drugged and controlled like that brought blurry tears to her eyes. She absolutely refused to entertain the horrible idea of them being assaulted the way Sam had described of that poor one worker lady.

Twice, they thought they were about to be discovered, but both times the worker went into the adjacent storage room to retrieve cleaning supplies. But slowly, the activity reduced to just the intermittent solitary worker carrying some item back to the pantry or putting away a broom. There was also the occasional booming shout of the Hive agent urging them to hurry up.

Finally, all went silent. Tiffany glanced over at Sam's watch: 8:00AM. Two hours wasted hiding in a closet. Their "prisoner" hadn't stirred, and Tiffany whispered, "You didn't kill him, did you?"

"No, his chest is rising and falling. He's alive," Sam assured. "Perhaps it had something to do with his drugged state making him sleep more soundly."

***

Finally after another ten minutes of making sure the coast stayed clear, Sam motioned for her to follow him. Tiffany gripped her rifle and headed out. Sam paused for a moment and looked back at the man still unconscious and zip tied to the workbench. Not knowing how long until he was discovered, and not wishing any real harm to come to him, Sam returned and set two water bottles next to him and closed the door.

Sam quickly checked both the kitchen and the pantry to be sure they were clear. They were. He ducked back in the pantry to grab a couple more bottles of water and apples, and then rejoined Tiffany in the hallway.

Except she wasn't there. He whispered her name as loudly as he dared. Nothing but silence. Dread filled him. He jerked open the door to both utility rooms ready to shoot some aggressor, but they were empty – except for their unconscious prisoner. He quickly checked the kitchen. She was nowhere to be found. The only place left to look was up the stairs.

He crept up the stairs. As he reached the top, he threw caution to the wind and sprinted down the hallway. As he passed the bathroom, he noticed the light was on. He skidded to a halt. Sam reached out and tried the handle, but it was locked.

"Tiffany," he whispered sharply.

The door opened and Tiffany's face stuck out. "What?" she whispered back.

"You can't just walk off like that," Sam said angrily.

"I had to go...bad," Tiffany explained. "We've been in here for like twelve hours and I've not gone once. I think that's a pretty big accomplishment for a woman. Now can I finish?"

Sam threw up his hands and motioned for her to hurry.

Inside the bathroom, Tiffany took a look at herself in the polished metal prison-style mirror. She looked dreadful. Her hair had been wet when she was kidnapped and so it had dried in the most despicable manner. She was filthy and had blood near her nose that she guessed was from running full speed into Sam's arm back in the compound. Never in her life had she wished more for a shower and a hairbrush.

She finished up and went to wash her hands, but then decided, as dirty as she was, what was the point. She exited the bathroom to a very annoyed Detective Cross.

"Seriously, don't just wander off like that again, understood? Or I'll handcuff you and leave you somewhere." Sam didn't really mean that; he was just angry and trying to make a strong point.

Tiffany sighed and nodded, and they continued down the hallway. Just for good measure they glanced in both the dining room and the dorm room to confirm they were indeed empty. There was also no sign of the Hive agent. Sam considered checking each floor to be sure he was gone, but decided against losing any more time. They headed for the front door.

Outside the coast looked clear. As Sam surveyed their surroundings, he saw where the Missing went. They were headed single file in two separate groups to the two large buildings they'd seen in the distance: the "stadium" and the "factory." Sam was shocked to see so many of them, but perhaps not as many as he had calculated – maybe only about 1000-1200. But still a lot. Sam ran the math through his head: ten buildings, each with beds for 204 people, so total capacity for just over 2000 people. Sam was pretty sure he wasn't looking at 2000 Missing. Which meant that some of the buildings either weren't full to capacity or perhaps were different kinds of buildings.

Tiffany jogged Sam out of his thoughts. "Where do you suppose they're going? And what are we going to do?"

Sam didn't answer right away but simply held up a finger indicating for her to wait a minute. Finally he spoke, "We have three courses of action to choose from. We could search the other eight buildings. But I'm not sure what we gain by doing so, other than confirmation that they match the two we've already searched. Or we could follow the Missing and try to figure out what kind of work exactly they're being used for. Or third, we could try to sneak back into the compound and see if we can get out of here."

"Well, it seems that most of the Hive agents are back in the compound," answered Tiffany, "So I vote *not* going that way."

"My thoughts exactly," Sam responded distractedly, still trying to think through their options.

"And," continued Tiffany, "I've seen enough of the inside of these apartment buildings, and I'm more curious about where all the Missing are going. Plus I want to see if we can find Laura…and maybe my mom."

Sam allowed his concentration to finally break. "Tiffany, I want you to prepare yourself for the likelihood that your friend and your mom are drugged like everyone else here. If we manage to find them, they won't recognize you until the drugs exit their system. And as with a lot of other psychotropic drugs, there may be a long and painful withdrawal period, depending on how long they've been forced to use them."

"I know." Tiffany bit her lip to keep tears back.

"Also," Sam continued, "should we find them, and I hope we do, you can't let emotion take over and endanger our chances of discovering what's going on here, bringing an end to it all, and getting out alive. Like when I saw that woman being assaulted earlier, the cop in me wanted to shoot him, tackle him – something to save her from the agent's violence. But ultimately it would've been very risky and likely led to our capture. The best way to save all of these people, including your mom and friend, is to bring down Hive."

Tiffany nodded, trying to keep a brave face despite the tears threatening to escape her eyes. She took a deep breath, squeezed her rifle tightly, and said, "Ok, let's do this."

The last of the Missing were almost inside the two buildings in the distance, and Sam was pretty sure he could see a few Hive agents bringing up the rear. Having decided to check out the "stadium" building first, Sam and Tiffany walked with a brisk pace down the path, keeping an eye out left, right, and occasionally behind them. It was eerily quiet. As they walked, Tiffany made a joke about walking down the "yellow brick road" to "see the wizard."

Sam was impressed by her strength – growing up under such oppression from Hive, losing her mother, losing her best friend, being literally dragged into all of this – not many women, or men even would still be able to crack a joke after all of that.

About ten minutes later, they arrived at the "stadium" building. The building was about twice the size of the "factory" building the opposite direction down the path. Now that he was closer, it more resembled a large aircraft hangar. Unfortunately, it didn't have any windows that he could see, which meant they were going to have to just enter and hope they didn't walk right into a load of Hive agents.

CHAPTER THIRTEEN
REVELATION

Madam Von Druska sat at her desk fuming. In her fourteen years as Grand Matron, the events of last night had been the biggest test of her leadership. She had been told by the previous and first Grand Matron who had groomed her to take over, stories of a handful of uprisings in the early years of Hamlin's occupation, but so far, except for during her transition, her administration had been uprising free. And overall, under her direction, Hive had prospered like never before. The number of Slaves she'd "acquired" meant plenty of free labor, minus feeding them of course. And as a result, Hive's operations had gone global. They were now the second largest black-market exporter of counterfeit merchandise behind the Chinese Triad. Their illicit drug manufacturing operation was edging out the rest of the North American market. And the relatively new operation of stealing and reselling exotic cars was a new bonus source of income – although after the appearance of Detective Sam Cross, she was strongly rethinking this new venture.

And really it didn't matter. Their latest breakthrough would make Hive and her, the wealthiest and most powerful secret organization in the world. Heck, if there were aliens out there somewhere, perhaps even in the universe.

For the first five decades of Hive's operation, the Slaves – or the "Missing" as the town's folk naively called them – had been controlled by fear through threats of death, solitary imprisonment, torture and attacks on their family. But then about a year ago, one of Hive's most brilliant chemists, in the process of trying to manufacture a new kind of illicit drug, had stumbled upon the formula for the serum. It was the perfect solution to controlling the Slaves. It could be easily injected, mixed with food – Hive had even experimented successfully with distributing it through a building's ventilation system.

Then about three weeks ago, one of Hive's global black market customers had visited the compound personally to try to broker a lucrative deal – well lucrative for him. Apparently, he thought his charm, and he did have a certain charisma about him, would make her cut him a special pricing deal. Little did he know that she cared nothing for cute smiles, chiseled physiques, and perfect hair. The previous Grand Matron, Madam Irina Jarik, had taught her that men only use women to prop themselves up, and she chose to honor the Grand Matron way of not taking a husband.

Madam Von Druska had lived here in the Hive compound for as long as she remembered. Madam Jarik had told her that her parents in Hamlin hadn't wanted her any longer and that Hive had graciously taken her in. Though she had believed that story during her childhood, she was no longer naïve enough to still believe it. Like many she'd taken during her leadership and turned into Slaves of Hive, no doubt she'd been taken from her parents. But it had been a blessed fate.

The people of Hamlin were weak. Hive had taught her strength, skill, and a better way of life than cowering like rodents along with the rest of her former people. She no longer considered herself one of them. They were just a means to an end – a façade of small-town life to provide cover for Hive's activities. Madam Jarik had been like a mother and mentor to her. Exactly why the former Grand Matron had chosen her specifically, she had never asked, but when Madam Jarik passed away fourteen years ago when Von Druska was only nineteen, she'd taken on the title of Grand Matron. The position, she had learned, came with absolute power. She got whatever and whoever she wanted.

She'd eyed a few of Hamlin's young girls – including Sheriff Gunn's daughter Tiffany, to take and raise to be the next in line of the Grand Matron succession, but honestly it was too soon. Von Druska was just thirty-three, so it would be another decade or so before she would need to get serious about finding her successor.

In any case, this wealthy customer had commented during his visit on how well-behaved and compliant the Slaves were. And he'd asked what control method Hive used. Von Druska had tried to avoid divulging the existence of the serum, but after he guessed at some kind of drug and then offered a ridiculous amount of money to buy in, she'd tentatively agreed. She'd explained to the potential buyer that present production levels of the serum were far too low for distribution to others – Hive had only enough on hand to supply its own personal needs. She'd proposed a six week timeline to increase their production levels and the buyer had eagerly agreed.

But things had gone better than anticipated. By next week, a whole two weeks early, the serum would be ready for distribution. Now if only she could catch this rat Detective, Hive would be richer and more powerful than ever. Her predecessor's dream had always been expansion to other cities, and now soon with the serum's power and the income it would generate, that dream would be realized.

The Grand Matron's daydreams of power and obscene wealth were interrupted by a knock at her door. She checked her appearance in the mirror on the back of the door and then answered.

***

Sheriff Gunn sat on Tiffany's bed with his head in his hands. As he thought over the last forty-eight hours, the puzzle pieces began to come together. Tiffany must've befriended and confided in Detective Cross. Tiffany had always been a strong-willed child, never one to just nod and smile and go with flow. She was a free-thinker; been that way all her life – just like her mother.

And it was that very spirit that had resulted in the loss of his sweetheart Alice. When Tiffany was just five years old, the former Grand Matron had died. Alice, who had already been holding secret Defiants meetings, as she called them, with others who hoped to take back Hamlin, saw the change in Hive leadership as their opportunity to fight back after decades of control.

But Hive had proved to be more informed than his wife had expected. Maybe there had been a Hive informant among the Defiants. Maybe Hive's surveillance had just been too prepared. In any case, the uprising during the leadership change had been a horrible failure. First, the Defiants' numbers had been too low – only about twenty. Second, their weapons had proven no match for those carried by Hive. Because of their black market activities, Hive had military grade weapons, and the shotguns and lever action hunting rifles of farmers and shopkeepers had been woefully inadequate.

And Madam Von Druska, the newly appointed Grand Matron, had been especially ruthless to the Defiants. Most of them had been massacred upon capture. But the Defiants leadership – which meant his Alice, had been taken, never to be seen again.

Sheriff Gunn had not joined in his wife's activities. Though he hated Hive, he wasn't the type to stage a protest. After the Defiants had been crushed, he'd tried to give up his post as sheriff, but the Grand Matron had cruelly refused his resignation. And she'd used his little Tiffany as a bargaining chip: stay as sheriff and do what he was told, or lose his daughter, too.

So now for nearly the last fifteen years, he'd done as he was told and Tiffany had been left alone to live a normal life – or at least Hamlin normal. She'd gone to school, gotten a job at Big-B Burger, and had a best friend. Then Laura went missing. Tiffany had begged him to do something, but he'd refused to talk about it, just like he did every time she brought up her mother.

Silence and compliance may have served him for the last fifteen years. But now the Grand Matron had broken their agreement – she'd taken Tiffany. The agents that came to his home earlier had not outright admitted that Tiffany had been taken by Hive, but they'd asked him when the last time he'd seen either Tiffany or Detective Cross. Plus who else would've drugged him. The agents had denied drugging him and suggested maybe he'd had one too many beers or fallen and hit his head, but Gunny knew that was a lie. He'd gone out to get Tiffany a pop and himself a beer and that was the last thing he remembered until Hive agents were splashing cold water on his face and peppering him with questions about his daughter and the detective.

He'd said that he wanted to go out and look for Tiffany. They'd said no. He'd demanded then to talk to the Grand Matron. And again they'd refused. And then they'd done the most ridiculous thing, barred him from leaving his home. And so here he sat, head in his hands on his daughter's bed – with zero answers and no tears left to cry.

Gunny stood up angrily. *I'll kill someone if they hurt Tiffany!* Gunny's thoughts of rage filled him. He turned and punched the back of Tiffany's door. He let out a string of curse words as the pain reverberated through his hand.

Gunny was tired of sitting, tired of crying, tired of rolling over, tired of playing the lap dog. It hadn't saved his wife; and now it had most likely cost him his daughter as well.

The last thing the Hive agents had done before they left was to take his service revolver. But they'd not even asked him about his other guns. Little did they know that his bedroom closet contained a small arsenal. Even Tiffany had never seen all his guns because he kept them behind the closet's back panel.

He had kept them mainly for his own amusement and private collection, never imagining he'd ever have a legitimate need for them – not being the Defiant type himself. But if ever there was a time and need, it was right now. Now in his room, he roughly pushed clothes aside in his closet. Behind them he gently moved the stack of framed family portraits he'd stored there since Alice disappeared. Seeing her beautiful smiling face and their little Tiffany all together as a family provided the final push he needed to do what had to be done.

It took him a minute to pry the tacks free that held the panel in place, but soon he was looking over his gun collection. He selected a pocket .380 pistol and then shoved a 1911 .40 caliber in his waistband. He grabbed a short-barrel 12-gauge shotgun and finally an AR-style rifle. Lastly he put on his hunting vest and filled it and every pocket on his jeans with ammo. Guns he had plenty of. Ammo not so much. Gunny didn't exactly count, but figured he had less than one hundred rounds.

He fitted the panel back in its spot, carefully rested the pictures against it, and shoved the clothes back in place. He chugged a can of beer for courage and moments later slid into his truck seat. Gunny fired up the engine and began rumbling down the gravel drive sending rocks shooting out behind from underneath the wheels.

As he drove, Gunny went over in his mind his plan. It wasn't elaborate at all. In fact, it was simple: bring home Tiffany by whatever means necessary. To be honest, Gunny wasn't sure if he could be successful but he figured he had the element of surprise, his love for his daughter, and a burning hot rage on his side. Those would have to be enough.

CHAPTER FOURTEEN
SABOTAGE

Tiffany swiped her badge at the “stadium” building and Sam looked cautiously through the crack in the door as he slowly pulled it open. His gun was at the ready. Though he had no way of knowing what awaited them inside, he was fully prepared to open up to a roomful of agents. Thankfully there were none, at least not yet in Sam’s view. With the door halfway open, he beckoned with his head for Tiffany to follow him inside.

They stepped inside to a small reception-like area. There wasn’t anything to see except another set of double doors. Like before, Tiffany reached up with her badge to swipe them in. Sam pulled on the door but it didn’t open. Sam looked at Tiffany and frowned. She reached up and swiped again, this time taking a closer look at the panel. Instead of the usual green light indicating a successful badge swipe, it flashed red.

Tiffany shrugged and whispered, “It’s not working. I’m just getting a red light.”

Sam frowned again. “That’s strange. This is the only door so far that’s not opened for us. I don’t like it. Try one more time.”

Tiffany swiped a third time and still nothing but a red light.

"Try your badge," she whispered back. Sam nodded and reached in his pocket.

***

Agent 15 was just walking out of the bathroom in the Assembly and Shipping Facility when the watch on his wrist illuminated. It signaled a front door panel fault. *Strange,* he thought and began walking toward the front door.

A moment later, his watch illuminated again signaling a second front door panel fault. He picked up the pace of his footsteps. "Why does there have to be a fault when I'm clear across the building," he muttered to himself.

Twenty seconds later, his watch illuminated for a third time indicating the same front door fault. He swore and broke into a run, while he began navigating through his smartwatch to signal the rest of the agents in the building to converge on the front door.

***

Sam fumbled through his cargo pockets trying to remember which pocket he'd put the badge in. Finally, he located it in his back left pocket and pulled it out. He handed it to Tiffany and took hers back in trade.

"Here's hoping," Tiffany whispered as she raised Sam's badge to the panel for a fourth swipe. The panel light lit green this time and the doors gave a faint click. "Success!" whispered Tiffany as Sam reached down to pull the door slowly open.

He glanced through the cracked door and seeing no one, motioned for Tiffany to follow him inside. They were now standing on a wide concrete floor that opened up to dozens of machines and assembly line conveyor belts. Along each side were the "residents" of Greytown working in robotic unison. Sam couldn't tell what they were assembling from where he stood, but whatever they were making, a lot of it was being produced with great efficiency.

Running in a big oval around the top of the building was a metal grate-style walkway. Ladders at various intervals led up to it. Sam guessed that's where the agents stood and oversaw the work being done.

Just then, Sam and Tiffany heard heavy footsteps pounding on the walkway above them getting louder and closer. Soon Sam could see an agent begin to rapidly descend one of the metal ladders. Just as Sam had feared, their failed keypad swipes had signaled Hive.

***

Just as Agent 15 hit the send button to signal the other agents in the building, his watch illuminated again. But this time, the message read, "FAULT CANCELED."

"Bah," spat Agent 15 as he skidded to a stop. Quickly he typed out a message of "False Alarm," to call off the other agents who would have just begun to respond.

The message came back: "Check to be sure."

"Roger," wrote back Agent 15. "But I'm not running anymore," he muttered under his breath.

"Agent 21 will accompany," came back the reply.

Agent 15 swung his foot over one of the ladders on the catwalk and began to descend to the bottom floor. He really didn't expect any trouble but it was definitely unusual that someone would've had a failed keycard swipe three times in a row.

Agent 15 cautiously approached the front door. No one was there. "Strange," he mumbled to himself, "there's no way someone could have slipped past me." He turned to look over his shoulder to see if Agent 21 was almost there, and then his world went black.

***

Sam and Tiffany had quickly made a plan to split up and hide in the shadows by the front door in case someone came. Sam would use his baton like before to hopefully incapacitate the guard as quietly as possible and without attracting any further attention.

The moment the Hive agent looked away, Sam stepped swiftly out of the shadows and swung his extended baton onto the back of the agent's neck. He crumpled to the ground. Sam bent down to drag the agent into the corner, but then he got that creepy feeling of being watched. Sam started to spin around, but was met with the barrel of a rifle.

Sam froze for a moment and then slowly stood up fully. He saw an open doorway in the wall that he'd evidently missed earlier. Another Hive agent had come through it and his rifle was now jammed into Sam's ribcage. Sam looked around quickly for Tiffany, but she was nowhere to be seen.

He hoped she was still hiding and that she'd stay that way. The Hive agent mistook Sam's looking around as a sign that he might run and growled, "Don't think about it. I haven't shot my weapon in a while and I'd love to break my cold streak on you. Just give me an excuse. You know I could've just done it anyway for you whacking Agent 15 like that. But the Grand Matron might want to do it herself, so I'll just take you in."

Sam remained silent, thinking the whole time of his next move. The agent gouged his ribs with the rifle. "Move it," he said gruffly and motioned in the direction of where Tiffany had been hiding. If Tiffany was discovered, Sam made up his mind to try and wrestle the rifle from the agent. "Let's go!" said the agent, annoyed at Sam's slow pace.

It took all of Sam's willpower not to look in the direction Tiffany had been hiding as they passed by, not wanting to give her position away. Sam hoped that she'd be smart enough not to try anything. If she fired her rifle, the whole place would be upon them. Sam would have to figure out his own escape…

Whack! Motion out of the corner of Sam's left eye made him duck instinctively. He spun around and at his feet lay the Hive agent. His rifle skidded across the floor. Over him stood a very angry and scared-looking Tiffany. She had rifle-butted the agent as hard as she could in the side of his head, knocking him to the ground. He wasn't entirely out, but was clearly in a ton of pain and dazed badly. Sam quickly grabbed Tiffany's rifle. And pointed it into the back of the agent's head.

"Give *me* a reason," Sam retorted.

Sam reached into his cargo pocket and pulled a pair of zip-cuffs he'd prepared from the zip ties he'd bought earlier and instructed Tiffany to cuff the agent behind his back. "Tight," Sam added. He then proceeded to duct tape the agent's mouth and together they dragged him over to the corner where Tiffany had been hiding.

Sam turned to Tiffany. “Impressive. And I appreciate that a lot,” he said with a smile.

“Any time,” she laughed nervously. Sam could see her hands shaking, but she looked proud of herself.

Sam quickly returned to the first guard and cuffed and duct taped him as well. Sam grew more uneasy by the minute. Things were quickly escalating. The disappearance of two guards wouldn’t go unnoticed for long. And Sam wasn’t even sure of the best place to hide them. He looked over at the hidden door through which he’d been ambushed by the Hive agent.

“Help me drag them in here,” Sam whispered.

A couple minutes later, both guards were in a small room – what looked like possibly a break room. “We’re in a pickle here,” Sam said. “These guards will be discovered missing before long, and they’re likely to be found pretty quickly in this room. It’s not gonna be long before we’re not a secret anymore.”

“So what are you saying?” asked Tiffany.

“I’m saying things might get really bad really fast,” replied Sam.

“Ok so what should we do? Go back outside? Or see where that door leads?” asked Tiffany pointing at the door on the opposite side of the small room. “Or go continue searching the main room?” Her voice trailed off.

“I think the main room is the best bet. I’d like to figure out where they’re manufacturing the serum and try to sabotage its production.” Sam’s voice took on a more serious tone. “I think we also need to come to grips with the high likelihood of not making it out of here."

"No, don't say that," Tiffany reassured. "You've been quite impressive so far."

Sam smiled grimly. "Well, so have you, but the fact remains that when I made up my mind to infiltrate Hive's base, I had no idea the size of their organization, the operations going on here – or heck, even the size of their base. I mean, not in a million years would I have guessed this drab Greytown existed behind a holographic wall. There's two of us; there's dozens if not hundreds of them. They have a powerful drug controlling the Missing to do their bidding – I'm just being honest. I think we've bitten off more than we can chew and I don't think just the two of us can put a stop to all of this *and* rescue hundreds of mind-controlled people."

Tiffany's eyes grew teary but she bit her lip to drive the tears back. She cleared her throat and said with a shaky voice, "So you're saying – go out guns blazing, cause what mayhem we can, and just see how far we can get?"

Sam smiled. "Something like that. I dunno about the guns blazing part – though it may come to that. I say, let's move fast, but still as silently as possibly. Let's see if we can find out where they're producing the serum. And then see if we can at least disrupt or ruin its production. It may not stop Hive permanently, but at least our time here won't be a waste. And then maybe do some blazing guns," Sam added with a wink.

"I wonder still," Tiffany mused, "if there's any chance of completely knocking out the serum's production to allow it to wear off in the Missing's bodies, and then gather them for an uprising."

"Maybe," replied Sam, "but I honestly don't see us disabling Hive's production here and then successfully hiding out for two days until the serum wears off without being caught first. But I suppose it's worth a try. Alright, enough talking. Let's get moving."

Sam and Tiffany exited the small break room back out the way they'd come. He'd taken the watch from one of the Hive agents. He'd noticed the communication ability of it and thought it might come in handy. Sam had never seen such a high-tech watch like that before. It looked like some kind of special ops military gadget.

As they exited the room, the watch Sam had taken suddenly lit up. "Agent 15. Agent 21. Status report," it read in bright red LED.

Sam didn't usually a cuss, but stress and exhaustion got the better of him and he let out an expletive under his breath. Tiffany turned and looked as Sam held up the watch.

"Well answer it," Tiffany said.

"I don't even know how to work this thing or what I'd say. What if they use some kind of code or lingo? Do I say 'all clear' or '10-4' or…?"

"Oh just give it here," Tiffany said and snatched it from Sam's hand.

"Wait," began Sam, but Tiffany was already pressing buttons rapidly on the keypad.

Sam tried to look and see what she was doing, but a moment later she handed the watch back to Sam with a smile. "All done," she announced. "It's just like texting."

Sam shot her an annoyed look. The screen read, "All good. Nothing to report."

"That'll work I suppose," he said.

"Maybe I should just hold onto it," said Tiffany with a touch of snark in her voice.

Unable to think of a reason why not, Sam reluctantly handed it back to her. Sam and Tiffany moved quickly down the right side of the building. So far, they had encountered no other Hive agents. *Wouldn't it be a stroke of luck if the two we tied up were the only ones watching the entire building?* Sam thought hopefully.

Sam motioned for Tiffany to hold up. About twenty-five feet or so in front of them, the building opened up more fully into a large assembly floor. Four rows of conveyor belts filled the open space, each side lined with the Missing. Sam's heart sank. The Missing here were making counterfeit merchandise for sale on the black market – not the serum as Sam hoped.

"Tiffany," Sam whispered, "I think we've got to go back out and make our way over to the other building. They're not making the serum here."

Tiffany crept forward for a closer look, ignoring Sam's instructions. She was just about to turn away, when she inhaled sharply and audibly. She started forward, but Sam grabbed her shoulder. "Where are you going?" Sam asked sternly.

Tiffany tore away from Sam. "It's Laura!" she exclaimed.

"Stop!" Sam ordered. "We talked about this. She's drugged. She won't recognize you. She's not in any danger and you can't help her by going to her. We have to stick to the plan."

"What plan?!" Tiffany spat angrily through tears. "Get ourselves caught? Go out guns blazing? Our plan sucks, and it doesn't help Laura either."

Sam just stood there for a minute and let her vent. Finally he answered gently, "I'm so sorry Tiffany. Sometimes the cop in me forgets to be human. I realize that this is your life, your family, and your town and that I'm an outsider here on a mission."

He paused for a moment to get a read on Tiffany, but she continued to glare, so he continued, "I'm sorry for not remembering you in all of this. You've been a huge help and I'm thankful for that. I don't want to fail at this any more than you do. And I promise you I'll do everything I can to make us succeed, if that's possible and save Laura and every other enslaved person here."

Tiffany stared at him, hands on her hips, but still said nothing.

"I really believe we need to get to the other facility and do something about the serum if we hope to have a chance at that. This is good actually. We know that Laura is alive and not in any immediate danger. So, let's get over to the other building and hope that it's the right one."

Tiffany still didn't answer, so Sam urged, "Okay?" And then he added, "Would a hug help?"

Tiffany sniffled and Sam saw her try to hide a smile. "Sure," she finally said.

After a few seconds, Tiffany straightened up and said wryly, "Stop wasting time being sensitive and let's get going."

Sam grinned and replied, "Okay tough girl."

They hurried back the way they'd come. Sam peaked inside the room where they'd left the bound agents. They were still there – and awake now – and super angry. But Sam had also zip-tied their feet, so all they could do was wriggle fruitlessly on the ground.

Sam waved and said, "You boys behave," and then he shut the door.

Sam and Tiffany exited the building and stepped back out into the drabness of Greytown. There wasn't a soul in sight, and so Sam and Tiffany opted for an open run down the path toward the "factory" building. The more Sam thought about it, the more he realized it would've made more sense for a building that looked like a factory to be where the serum was made rather than the "stadium" building they'd just left.

But lesson learned. About halfway to the "factory" Tiffany motioned for them to slow down.

"Phew, I need to drink fewer sodas and get my butt off the couch more," Tiffany huffed. "Plus this rifle is heavy," she added.

"No worries," Sam reassured. "We can speed-walk the rest of the way there. We also ought to save some strength and not be out of breath when we arrive at the next facility. Who knows what we'll face there – and it's hard to be quiet when you're sucking for air."

About ten minutes later they arrived at the front entrance of the "factory." Sam reached up his keycard and gave it a swipe. The panel illuminated green on the first try and he cautiously opened the door while Tiffany held her rifle to cover.

Sam ducked his head inside, but like at the "stadium" the coast was clear. He held the door for Tiffany to go first and inside they went.

CHAPTER FIFTEEN
ATTACK!

Gunny looked back at the ruts he'd just made in his drive. He and Tiffany would rake them out when he had her back home safe and sound, he thought with a smile.

Gunny drove into town, careful not to speed – not knowing what Hive agents might be watching him. He actually didn't see any. *They're probably busy still searching for Detective Cross,* Gunny thought. In town, he made his way first quickly to his office. He was pretty sure he had a box of shotgun shells there in his desk.

He did indeed and hurried back outside after retrieving them. Next he made his way across the street to the hardware store. The store was open, but Mr. Thompson wasn't immediately visible. "Jim," Gunny yelled. "Get out here man."

Jim hurried out in his usual nervous manner. "What is it, Gunny? Can I get you something?"

"Bullets – all you got," Gunny said impatiently.

"But you know I ain't got no ammo," Jim stammered.

"Would you like to get a speeding ticket every day for the rest of your life or would you like to give me that ammo I know you've got behind the counter in that little safe?" Gunny answered menacingly.

"Oh, that ammo," Jim answered, his eyes looking downward in the safe's direction.

"Jim, they've got Tiffany," Gunny said, his voice cracking ever so slightly. "So for once in your life, can you just do something that helps somebody beside yourself? Please?"

Wordlessly, Jim bent down and with shaking hands spun the dial to unlock the safe. "I've got 9mm, some .40, and a few rounds of .223. I haven't got any shotgun shells, so sorry about that."

"What you got will be just fine," Gunny said impatiently.

Gunny grabbed the ammo boxes and turned to rush out of the store. He paused with the door halfway open. "Thank you Jim. And if you are that type – would you say a prayer for my Tiffany." He left before hearing Jim's answer.

From the hardware store, Gunny hurried back to his truck. He headed from there to Mrs. Gena's. About five minutes later he pulled in the drive and walked quickly to the front door. He stepped inside hollering for Mrs. Gena.

"Oh, there you are," Gunny said, noticing her in the foyer chair. He started to ask about the detective and his daughter when he noticed the scared look in her eyes. Gena wasn't looking at him, but at something behind him. Gunny decided to play it cool.

He walked toward her and asked casually, "I was headed down to the office, but I thought about your Hamlin-famous cookies and thought I'd swing by to see if you had any."

"Oh, you're too sweet Gunny," Mrs. Gena replied weakly

Gunny noticed the large, fresh bruise on her right arm, but kept talking naturally. "Not as sweet as those cookies though," he said with his big smile. "Don't get up. If you'll just tell me where they are, I'll go fetch them myself."

Gena caught Gunny's hint. "They're in my office. I hadn't set them out yet," she replied, signaling the location of the hidden Hive agent.

Gunny decided on a bit of misdirection. "Oh, can I use your restroom first – that burger I had for lunch isn't setting right."

Gena nodded. Gunny, headed for the restroom, but instead ducked into the parlor beside the piano. "I'll be out in just a minute and then get those cookies and be on my way," Gunny called. He hoped the Hive agent would come out while he was in the "restroom."

It worked. The agent exited the office and walked over to Gena. "I know what you were trying to do," the agent said gruffly. "There aren't any cookies in your office. You think you're smart, but you're just a stupid, old…"

His voice trailed off as he felt the cold steel of Gunny's .40 behind his left ear. "I wouldn't finish that sentence if I were you," Gunny warned.

"Now Sheriff, don't do anything stupid," the agent threatened.

"I'm well beyond stupid at this point," Gunny said "Where's my daughter – and choose your words carefully."

The agent didn't respond, so Gunny kicked him in the back of the knees making the agent's knees bend and him buckle to the ground. Gena let out a gasp.

"If you think I'm screwing around, just ignore me one more time," Gunny said coldly.

The agent remained silent.

"Mrs. Gena you might wanna step away. And I'm sorry about your floor. I promise to clean it up and fix any damages when I get back with Tiffany."

Gena's eyes grew wide and she painfully began to pull herself out of the chair.

"Alright!" exclaimed the Hive agent. Gena lowered herself back in the chair.

"She was taken to the Grand Matron," the agent admitted.

"And?" pressured Gunny.

"And then I don't know what happened," the agent replied. "She never arrived. I think that Detective had something to do with it. We found one of our agents tied up outside the gate. She was never transferred to the hold like she was supposed to be. That's why they've got us searching door to door across the town."

"Then why aren't you helping?" Gunny asked.

"I was left here in case they came back," answered the agent. "But I've not seen them. And I'm guessing they've still not been found or they'd have signaled me."

Gunny thought for a minute. So, Tiffany *had* been taken, but Cross had most likely rescued her. Not sure how he'd pulled that off, but Gunny didn't care – just so long as Tiffany was safe. But where could they be hiding out? There were no Defiants left that Gunny knew of. And Hamlin was only so big. Maybe in the woods by the park? Or in the high school? Gunny wasn't sure, but he had a decision to make – search the town on his own and try to find them first or make his way to the Hive base.

***

Sam and Tiffany crept carefully into the "factory" building. Since they hadn't used the wrong keycard this time, no one had been alerted to their presence. The layout of this building wasn't as open as that of the "stadium." And there was no catwalk running above.

Sam froze as Tiffany patted his arm and pointed. About ten yards away was a very bored looking Hive agent sitting in a chair that thankfully hadn't noticed them yet. Sam pondered their next move. He didn't like the out-in-the-open position of where the agent was sitting because silencing him would mean exposing himself. But Sam wasn't sure there was any choice if they were to proceed.

An idea popped into his head. It was a bold one, but the only thing he thought might work. He handed Tiffany his pistol and motioned for her to give him her rifle. And then he put on the ski mask Tiffany had taken from the Hive agent at the gate after Sam rescued her.

He slung the rifle over his shoulder and made a "how do I look" gesture? Tiffany shrugged, confused.

"Do I look like I could pass as an agent of Hive?" he whispered.

"Oh, yeah I guess, maybe at first glance," she answered.

"A moment of deception is all I need, so I'm good then. Stay here," he ordered and then walked directly toward the guard.

Tiffany watched nervously from the shadows.

About fifteen feet from the agent sitting watch, Sam called out, “Hey, need you to come help me with something. HQ wants us to search the building for the missing girl.”

The agent stood to his feet and started toward Sam. “I wasn’t told about it. Who’s taking my spot here?” the agent challenged, still approaching Sam.

The distance closed between them quickly. Suddenly when the agent was about four feet from Sam, the agent realized that Sam wasn’t a fellow Hive member.

“Hey!” he began, but it was too late. Sam’s baton extended swiftly and found its mark perfectly on the side of the agent’s head.

With a soft groan, the agent’s knees buckled and he fell to the ground motionless. Sam looked around quickly and then dragged the agent back in the direction toward Tiffany.

She sprang toward Sam to give him a hand. Soon the unconscious agent was zip-cuffed and duct taped securely.

Sam began patting down the agent’s pockets. He felt something cylindrical in one of the cargo pockets. He pulled it out to discover that it was four vials of clear liquid, each with a needle taped to the side.

Sam held it up for Tiffany to see. Her eyes grew wide. “Serum,” she whispered.

“Yup, and this just might come in handy,” Sam said with a grin.

“How so?” she asked. “I thought we were trying to undo the zombie effect, not create it.”

"I'd like to see what happens if I shoot up a Hive agent with this stuff," Sam whispered back.

"Nice one," Tiffany said, grinning.

Sam thought for a second and then made a suggestion. "This agent is on the smaller side. I think it might be a good idea for you to change into his uniform."

Tiffany nodded and helped Sam remove the agent's pants, trying not to look at the half-naked agent.

Tiffany whispered, "I think the pants will be enough. I have the other Hive agent's jacket on."

Sam nodded and motioned for her to change. Tiffany paused and looked around for a private place. "There's no ladies room," Sam said amused. "I'll just stand watch and you change behind me as fast as you can.

If Tiffany had felt awkward undressing the Hive agent, now she *really* felt awkward undressing with Sam only a couple feet away. The pants were too big of course for her twiggy frame, but she cinched up the belt and rolled the pant legs a couple times.

Tiffany walked into Sam's view and gave him the same "how do I look" gesture he'd given her earlier. Sam smiled and gave her a thumbs up. Tiffany removed the agent's watch and stuck it in her pocket. That way if the guard they'd just taken down received a message, she could respond to it.

Sam looked at his watch impatiently. He knew that their time grew shorter by the minute and that it was only a matter of time before the now three agents they'd recently incapacitated were discovered and their cover blown.

He motioned for Tiffany to follow him and moved forward.

The foyer opened up into a large room like before in the "stadium" though quite a bit smaller. Its assembly line was also completely different. And the room smelled medicinal. This was without a doubt where the serum was made. A couple hundred of the Missing worked mindlessly filling, sealing, and labelling vials of clear liquid like those in Sam's pocket.

He quickly surveyed the room. The only other Hive agent that Sam could see was behind a glass window in a room off to the side. One wall inside the room had a large computer panel on it – perhaps controlling the pumps and other equipment that the Missing were using to manufacture and bottle the serum.

Sam couldn't imagine what Hive would want so much serum for – there was far more being made than what he supposed would be needed to control the Missing.

Sam and Tiffany waited until the agent in the side room looked over at the panel and then dashed quickly along the wall in his direction. Sam saw the agent suddenly look down to the watch on his wrist, and at the same time the watch in Tiffany's pocket vibrated.

Tiffany pulled it out and they looked at the message together in horror: "Agents down in Building 14. All agents immediately report their number and position."

They'd been discovered!

Sam had no idea what the agent numbers were of the watches they'd taken. He knew one of them was either fifteen or twenty-one. But the agent they'd just knocked out – Sam had no clue what his number was.

Sam chose to ignore responding and moved quickly with Tiffany in tow toward the room with the agent in it. The agent inside noticed them, but just stared. At the door of the room, Sam tried his keycard. It didn't work. Tiffany quickly tried hers. It didn't work either.

The agent inside made a confused gesture. Sam shrugged and mimed with his hands for the agent to open the door. The agent did, though somewhat cautiously.

With the door ajar only a couple inches, the agent asked, "What's up with your badges?"

Sam didn't respond, but instead lunged toward the door trying to force his way inside. The agent was much larger than Sam and he threw his weight back against the door trying to close it. Sam's foot kept it open.

"Who are you?" the agent shouted with a grunt. Tiffany joined in and threw her small frame against the door and it began to budge open.

A look of recognition crossed the agent's face. He tried to hold the door with his body and his foot while at the same time sending out a signal with his watch.

He was able to quickly type out, "Serum Room. Come."

Sam let out a roar and shoved the door as hard as he could, finally forcing his way inside. However the door closed before Tiffany could follow. She was stuck outside.

***

Tiffany watched helplessly as Sam and the agent struggled inside. Sam was clearly the better fighter, but the agent had the size advantage – and apparently was able to take a beating and keep fighting.

Suddenly Sam's footing slipped, and the agent quickly grabbed him from behind in a chokehold. Tiffany screamed. Sam struggled, but it was obvious to Tiffany that he was moments from passing out or being killed.

Tiffany looked around frantically for some way to break inside. Then she remembered her rifle. She pulled it from her back and took aim at the glass window and fired four shots. The glass exploded and the Hive agent dove for cover under the desk. Sam lay unconscious on the floor.

Tiffany paused to consider her options and then aimed the rifle at the control panel on the wall. She squeezed off several rounds and the panel shattered like the glass moments ago before catching on fire. The assembly machinery behind her skidded to a stop. From the corner of her eye she could see the Missing standing in apparent confusion at having their work interrupted.

Tiffany yelled as fiercely as she could muster at the agent. "Get up and open this door. Now!"

The agent scurried out from under the desk. He paused briefly and looked at his rifle, but the enraged look on Tiffany's face caused him to reconsider. He opened the door and stepped back.

"On your knees, face the wall," she ordered. The agent complied, wincing as he knelt in broken glass.

"This whole place is about to be overrun with the might of Hive. You've made a huge mistake," the agent jeered.

"Shut up!" Tiffany shouted.

Keeping an eye on the kneeling agent, she took Sam's pistol and set the rifle down. She also pulled the duct tape and a pair of zip-cuffs from Sam's pocket. Cautiously, she approached the agent.

"Hands behind your back," she ordered.

She slid the zip-cuffs on the agent's wrists and cinched them tight. Not wanting to take any chances, she began wrapping the duct tape rapidly and wildly around the agent's head.

Suddenly he lunged toward her. He was blinded however by the duct tape over his eyes and missed with his attack. Tiffany sprang back and while the blinded agent tried to find her, she grabbed the rifle against the wall and bashed him repeatedly in the face until he stopped moving. From under the tape on his face, blood began to appear.

She hoped he wasn't dead, but at the same time, at that moment, she didn't exactly care. She now turned her attention to Sam, shaking him and gently patting his face to try and rouse him. He didn't move. Spotting a bottle of water on the desk, she snatched it up and quickly began pouring it on Sam's face and the back of his neck. The cold water eventually caused Sam to begin to stir and finally sit up.

Sam opened his eyes and blinked several times. He rubbed his eyes and looked around. His eyes grew wide at the sight of the smoldering control panel, the broken glass window, and the motionless, bleeding agent nearby.

"You did all this," Sam asked in amazement as he struggled to gain his feet, slipping on broken glass.

"I had to save you," she replied warmly.

Sam gave her a hug and tousled her hair. "I owe you one – a big one," he said.

"We have to hurry," Tiffany said grimly. "The agent said that he got a message out and that all of Hive would be here soon. I was hoping he was bluffing, but it's right here on the watch in my pocket."

"Well, the busted panel will stop production for a little bit, but I wager they'll have it back up and running before too long," Sam said, still trying to clear his foggy brain.

"I say let's just shoot up as much equipment as we can then. Break as many vials of serum as possible in the process. Guns blazing right?" Tiffany said picking up the agent's bloodied rifle.

"Works for me. But listen, when they tell us to surrender, don't fight. As long as we're alive, there's hope," Sam urged.

Tiffany nodded.

Quickly grabbing the rifle Tiffany had dropped earlier, he patted down the agent and found two spare magazines in his cargo pocket.

"Let's do this. But careful not to shoot any of the Missing," Sam said as they left the room.

Sam and Tiffany headed in opposite directions toward various pieces of the assembly equipment. Tiffany heard Sam fire the first shot and she followed, sending a spurt of bullets into the machine in front of her. She next fired at one of the filling stations causing the clear serum to ooze out. With the side of her rifle, she ran it over the lined up bottles of serum on the conveyor belt, knocking them to the floor and crushing hundreds in the process.

The Missing, disturbed by the noise and mayhem, had moved to a huddled mass back toward the front door. Lined up at the rear of the building, Sam encountered several pallets stacked with boxes marked "ZS-37" – likely the real name for the serum. He fished in his pocket for the lighter he'd taken from the first agent back at the gate, now what seemed like so long ago. He wedged it between two of the boxes, aimed his handgun at it, and fired. It burst into flames, quickly catching the boxes on fire.

Sam scanned for another target. As he did, he looked at the damage they'd caused. Crushed vials and sticky serum covered the floor. Machinery sparked and smoked. His eyes traced the piping upwards to a large holding tank mounted from the ceiling – likely a stock tank full of serum.

Sam shouted for Tiffany to join him back in the control room. Once they were both inside, Sam and Tiffany took aim at the stock tank and fired their weapons. Like a cloud releasing a downpour of rain, serum cascaded to the floor.

Just then light shown from the front door and dozens of agents poured inside the room, pushing their way through the frightened, huddled Missing. Sam stopped firing and laid his rifle down, motioning for Tiffany to do the same. He brushed a spot free for himself and Tiffany to sit not in glass, and then rested against the wall, hands on his head. Tiffany followed his example. Moments later Sam and Tiffany were face down in glass, cuffed, and then dragged from the room.

They were dropped on the floor before a pair of glossy boots. An agent jerked them up by their hair to their knees, and Sam and Tiffany looked through bloodied faces into the eyes of the livid Grand Matron.

CHAPTER SIXTEEN
GUNNY

As Gunny pondered his next move, the watch on the agent's wrist lit up. What he read made him feel momentarily ill. "All agents report to base. Threat neutralized."

Gunny let out an anguished roar. "What does that mean?" he demanded.

"It means your stupid daughter and that rogue detective got caught – or killed," he answered wickedly.

Enraged, Gunny whipped his pistol across the back of the agent's head, causing it to bleed.

"You fool," the agent spat. "You thought the three of you could defeat Hive?"

Gunny kicked the agent in the middle of the back and jumped on him, driving his knee into the spot he'd just kicked. He shoved his gun into the back of the agent's bloodied head.

"I'd kill you right now but my Alice wouldn't want me to," Gunny grunted through clenched teeth.

Instead, he cuffed him, and dragged him toward the front door.

"Sorry about the mess Mrs. Gena. I'll fix it when I get back." And then he and the agent stumbled out the front door. Gunny shoved the agent toward the passenger side of the truck and ordered him to climb into the backseat. He laid the shotgun and his rifle on the floorboard in the front just to be sure the agent didn't try anything, and then headed for the driver's side.

"You're gonna help me get inside that compound, and if you screw with me at all, I won't hesitate to kill you," Gunny warned.

The agent apparently realized that Gunny wasn't bluffing and sat quiet and still in the backseat for the short drive to the junkyard. At the gate, Gunny demanded, "Passcode." The agent motioned with his head toward the breast pocket of his jacket and Gunny reached in and found a keycard.

The gate slid open and Gunny's truck rumbled inside. From the guard shack to his right emerged an agent. The agent, rifle aimed at the truck, began to move round toward the driver's side. This proved to be a poor choice because as soon as he stepped in front of Gunny's truck, the sheriff jammed the gas, running the cattle guard on his truck into the agent. Gunny felt the thud of the agent's body and then jammed the brakes.

He exited the truck to see the agent's mangled body under his bumper. Gunny took the fallen agent's rifle and then dragged his limp form back toward the guard shack. Once the body was hidden inside, he jogged back over to the truck to find the agent trying to climb over the seat. Gunny pointed the dead agent's rifle at him, and he slowly slid back into his seat.

Gunny went around to the passenger side of the truck and opened the door. "Actually, I don't need you anymore. Get out of there," Gunny ordered, but the agent sat frozen in fear.

"Don't make me shoot you in my truck," Gunny warned, and the agent slowly slid out. Gunny ordered him into the guard shack, trying to think of what to do with both agents. The safest would be just to shoot them both, but Gunny didn't want that on his conscience since neither were an actual threat at the moment.

"Y'all got any handcuffs in here?" Gunny asked.

The agent motioned toward a vest on the wall. Inside, among other things, were two pairs of handcuffs. Gunny ordered the agent to lie down on his face, and then Gunny cuffed his feet. He looked over at the agent he'd run over and considered cuffing him as well, but the way he looked, it wasn't likely he'd cause any trouble. So Gunny used the second pair of cuffs to hobble the agent he'd just cuffed. With the butt of the rifle, he then smashed all the computers and comms equipment before closing the door and heading back to his truck.

Gunny rumbled forward toward the two buildings at the back of the compound. At the hangar-style building he exited his truck again and peered through the door. To his surprise it was deserted. Gunny drove over to the office-looking building on the compound's left where he usually met with Agent Grant. Using the keycard from the guard, he entered the building.

He rapidly descended down the stairs. At the end of the familiar hallway, he entered the large room where he usually waited to meet Agent Grant – and where he'd recently met with the Grand Matron. Gunny looked around and saw no one. He did notice that the gun rack that usually held several rifles was empty. Instead of waiting as usual, Gunny walked toward the door on the right where Agent Grant always entered and exited. Another swipe of the keycard and Gunny was inside. There was a hallway on the other side with five doors on the right and one door at the end of the hall. Gunny checked them in order as he moved down the hall. They were all empty.

The room at the end of the hallway was the only one his keycard would not open. On the door was Hive's emblem. Perhaps this was the Grand Matron's quarters. Gunny threw his large frame at the door and it burst open destroying the doorframe in the process. Looking around, he was sure he was standing in the Grand Matron's personal quarters.

Gunny looked back down the hallway behind him, wondering where everyone was – he wasn't exactly being quiet. The agent at Mrs. Gena's had said that all of Hive had been summoned to the base and there was no way he'd beaten them back.

Gunny exited the room and began down the hallway, but near the end he halted. Back in the Grand Matron's room, he'd seen a desk with a phone and other communication equipment on it. Surely if anyone had the ability to contact the outside world, it would be the Grand Matron. "You're a big ol' boy," Gunny said to himself, "but you could use some help." He jogged back to the room.

As he hunched over the desk it occurred to Gunny – he had no idea who to call. He'd never made a long-distance call before. He had no other law enforcement contacts. He dug through the desk drawers looking for ideas. Under a locked metal box, Gunny found an address book. Inside were all kinds of phone numbers – some with weird prefixes that he guessed were for international numbers.

One contact caught his eye: "OKC Cars." Detective Cross had mentioned he was from Oklahoma City and that he had come to look for a stolen car. Maybe this was the Grand Matron's contact for her car operation in OKC. Gunny of course couldn't call the actual number, but he had something now to go on – the prefix numbers for OKC: 405. Gunny picked up the phone on the desk and was greeted with a good sign – a dial tone. He dialed "405" and then a random string of numbers.

They were apparently the wrong ones because he got a weird tone and then a recorded voice saying, "We're sorry. The call cannot be completed as dialed. Please check the number and dial again."

Gunny swore under his breath and tried another set of numbers. This one rang. Gunny waited impatiently for someone to pick up. However it rang four times and then went to voicemail. Gunny considered leaving a voice message – but what would he say that wouldn't sound crazy? He hung up and tried a third number.

After two rings, a woman's voice answered, "Thank you for calling Mark and Son's Tires. Would you like to speak to sales or the service department?"

Gunny spoke earnestly, "Listen ma'am, this is Sheriff Paul Gunn of the Hamlin Oklahoma Police Department. This is an emergency. I need the number to the Oklahoma City Police Department immediately."

The woman's voice on the other end stuttered, "Uh, I…I'm sorry Sheriff, but I don't know that number off the top of my head. Did you try calling 911?"

"Listen lady," Gunny said sternly. "I'm in the middle of nowhere. I've got a real bad situation here and I need you to find me that phone number. Now. No matter what you have to do."

"I'm sorry. Yes sir," the woman said nervously on the other end of the line. "Let me just look it up here on my phone real fast."

Gunny bounced his knee anxiously as he waited. Seconds seemed like an eternity. "Hurry miss," Gunny implored.

"Just a second. Yes, here it is." The lady read the number to Gunny and he wrote it down on his hand and then repeated it back.

"You're absolutely sure that's it?" Gunny asked.

"Yes sir, I'm reading it right here off of their website," the woman answered.

"Got it. Thanks. Bye." And Gunny hung up the phone. He then quickly dialed the number.

"Oklahoma City Dispatch. Sergeant Halsey speaking, how can I help you?"

Gunny took a deep breath, knowing what he was about to say would probably sound insane. "This is Sheriff Paul Gunn of the Hamlin Police Department. I have your Detective Sam Cross here with me, and I need to speak to your chief at once. This is a life-or-death situation."

"Alright Sheriff Gunn. What's the best number to reach you at if we get cut off?" the dispatcher asked.

"I have no idea," Gunny said annoyed. "I'm not in my office. If we get disconnected *I'll* call you back. Just get your chief on the phone."

"Yes sir, I'll see what I can do. Please hold," the dispatcher said and then the line went quiet.

A couple agonizing minutes ticked by, and finally the line came to life again. "This is Captain Durant. Who did you say you were?"

"I'm Sheriff Paul Gunn of Hamlin, Okla –" began Gunny.

Captain Durant cut him off, "Hamlin, you say? I was just there early this morning. My sergeant here tells me that you've seen my Detective, Sam Cross? He's been missing for a day and a half."

"Yes Detective Cross is here," Gunny replied. "And he's in danger. We all are. I need every police officer you can round up to come to Hamlin right away. Our town is under attack."

There was a long pause on the other end of the line. "Hello?" Gunny asked.

"I was just there and spoke to one of your officers early this morning. They were cleaning up a traffic accident on the road leading into town. But they assured me that my Detective had not been in Hamlin."

"Those were Hive, not police officers. I'm the only law enforcement in town," Gunny answered.

"Who's Hive? And what do you mean you're under attack?" Captain Durant asked.

Gunny narrowed his eyes in thought and then spoke. "This is gonna be the craziest story you've ever heard, but I swear on my wife's life that it's true. About fifty years ago this criminal militia group called Hive came into our town and took over. And ever since, they've been controlling our town – running some kind of criminal enterprise – I don't know what all. That missing car Detective Cross was looking for, was most likely stolen, and brought here to be shipped overseas. And ever since the Takeover, Hive has been kidnapping the folks of Hamlin and making them into who knows what. And now they've taken my daughter and your detective. And this place is about to come unglued at the seams in the firefight of the century. It's just me against them. And I need backup before we're all killed."

"You're right, Sheriff," answered Captain Durant after a deep breath. "That is the craziest thing I've ever heard – but since you know about Detective Cross, and since our last radio call from him was outside your city – I'm inclined to believe you even if what you say sounds like a TV show or something. So just hang tight Sheriff. We are your brothers in blue. Help is on the way."

"Thank God!" exclaimed Gunny. "Listen now. Don't trust anyone. I might be dead when you get here. But anyone telling you they're a police officer or an agent of the government that you don't know personally is Hive. If I happen to still be alive, you can't miss me. I'll be the biggest son of a gun you've ever seen and the only one of them with a moustache. Especially don't listen to a short middle-aged woman – she's their leader, Madam Von Druska." He took a quick breath and then continued, "If you happen to come across my daughter Tiffany, she's nineteen, skinny, and feisty as heck. You can also trust the old lady at the bed and breakfast – Mrs. Gena."

"Now how many of these, what'd you call them, Hive agents, did you say there were?" Captain Durant asked.

"I don't rightly know – but a small army; probably seventy-five or a hundred of them. I don't know. Just bring the cavalry," Gunny said.

Just then, Gunny heard the door to the hallway open and footsteps headed his way. "Shoot! They're coming. I've gotta go. When you get here, go to the city dump. It's a front for their base, no matter what else anyone tells you." And then Gunny hung up the phone.

Gunny turned toward the doorway, his .40 in his right hand and the .380 in his left. He hid behind the door frame, listening as the footsteps got closer.

***

"Hello? Sheriff Gunn?" Captain Durant said to the dead phone line.

"Trace that number," he ordered the desk sergeant. "Alright everyone, listen up. I think we've found Detective Cross. Officer Forrester, get me State Police on the phone. Detective Gill, call Cross's wife."

Son of a gun, thought Captain Durant. *What a wild story. What on earth did Sam get himself into?*

"State Police on Line 4, Captain Durant," said Officer Forrester.

He grabbed the phone and spoke to the Trooper on the line, "Yes this is Captain Durant, OKC Police Department. You're not gonna believe what I'm about to tell you, but I need your help in a big way…"

CHAPTER SEVENTEEN

GUNS BLAZING

Grand Matron Von Druska unholstered her sidearm in a deliberately slow and menacing way. She pointed it at the middle of Sam's forehead. Tiffany let out a terrified gasp. The Grand Matron moved the gun to her head instead and spoke coldly.

"I once considered you for my protégé, but looking at you now, I see that would've been a colossal mistake. You think you're strong and brave, but you're just a weak, stupid girl. Some other fortunate girl will be chosen when the time is right."

"What shall we do with these two pests?" the Grand Matron asked to nobody in particular. She re-holstered her weapon. "Death is too easy of a punishment."

Still staring down at Sam and Tiffany she said, "You've cost me millions with your stupidity. It will take weeks to get this back up and running. But this is your failure: you've neither stopped Hive's reign nor my plan for globalization – merely delayed it. What you've done here is only a minor inconvenience, one that will soon be corrected."

Agent Grant stepped up and spoke through his usual devilish grin. "They were found with these vials of the ZS-37 in the Detective's pocket," Agent Grant said, holding them up. "Mindless slavery – perhaps even personal slaves to you, seems like a fate worse than death."

Von Druska took the vials thoughtfully from Agent Grant. "Yes," she said with a deliberate pause. "It's a fitting start to a lifetime of retribution. The pests become the pets. And I believe I'll have you begin it now."

Having said so, she affixed a needle to one of the vials. Her eyes shifted between Sam and Tiffany as a child might choose between friends in a game. And then in a violent, swift downward swing, the Grand Matron impaled the needle into the side of Sam's neck.

Sam flinched and grunted in pain from the forceful injection. The drug was fast-acting. Almost at once Sam felt the serum's effects kick in. He had never done any kind of illicit drugs before, but the feeling of mental fogginess he was currently experiencing was exactly what he would've imagined drugs would feel like. Through the fog overtaking his mind, Sam heard Tiffany sob and scream in rage. He tried to mumble words of comfort, but Sam wasn't sure if he succeeded. His last thought before his mind completely left him was of his wife Jennifer and their two boys.

***

Through eyes blurred by angry tears, Tiffany watched as the serum overtook Sam's mind and his eyes took on the blank stare of the Missing. She was surprised that she didn't feel the least bit afraid as she watched the Grand Matron prepare another needle and vial for her own neck.

With the task complete, the Grand Matron looked at Tiffany with pure evil in her eyes. Just then her watch buzzed. It read: "Sector 1 access."

"Madam!" exclaimed Agent Grant. "Someone unauthorized just entered your quarters."

The Grand Matron looked at Tiffany, eyes narrowing. "We have another pest I see. I do believe it's time for a new sheriff in town."

Tiffany braced for the Grand Matron to inject her as well, but she instead turned and quickly walked away. Handing the serum to a nearby agent, she called over her shoulder, "Bring them both!"

Tiffany's mind raced. Could it really be her dad? Last she'd seen him, he'd been unconscious on their living room floor. She hadn't known whether he was dead or alive, but the Grand Matron's words gave her hope.

She was also worried for him. Her dad was a big man – perhaps the biggest in town and quite the intimidating presence – but could he succeed where she and Sam had failed? She shot a look over her shoulder. Sam followed, but she could tell by his eyes that Detective Sam Cross was gone.

Outside the building, Tiffany was shoved into an ATV-type vehicle and they followed at break-neck speed behind the Grand Matron's jeep. It took them less than five minutes to reach the false wall that exited Greytown. Tiffany instinctively flinched as they drove through it. The ATV she was riding on parked near the Hive barracks adjacent to the front gate. From there Tiffany spotted her dad's truck parked cockeyed near the building on the far left.

Shouts from the guard shack nearby drew her attention. Two agents carried an unconscious third agent outside and laid him on the ground. *Score one for Dad,* Tiffany thought. A few moments later another agent emerged as well, this one walking, but with a pronounced limp – also probably thanks to her dad.

Tiffany felt hope growing in her chest – if her dad could get inside the compound, incapacitate two agents, and then gain access to the Grand Matron's quarters, maybe there was a chance her dad could rescue her. All she could do was wait – and pray. Tiffany thought of Mrs. Gena and hoped she was praying as well.

***

Captain Durant raced down I-40 West out of Oklahoma City. Behind him followed over fifty patrol cars. Behind those, followed the OKC Tactical Response Team and a dozen ambulances – in case things went sideways. He looked at his watch. It would be a couple hours before they'd arrive in Hamlin – and if they were lucky it'd all be over before then. The Assistant Director of the Oklahoma Highway Patrol had redirected all Troopers within one hundred miles to converge on Hamlin. Captain Durant had also coordinated with the Oklahoma State Bureau of Investigations and the Oklahoma division of the Bureau of Alcohol Tobacco and Firearms – and they too were sending federal agents.

Unfortunately, his officers and the feds both had the long drive from OKC. State Troopers would be first on the scene – but based upon Sheriff Paul Gunn's description of a militia type gang, the troopers likely wouldn't move in until they'd amassed a sufficient assault force.

His radio squawked with the report of the first Highway Patrol to enter Hamlin.

***

Taking a quick glance into the hallway outside the Grand Matron's chambers Gunny saw two Hive agents running down the hallway, their black boots thundering as they drew nearer. About twenty feet from the door, they slowed to a cautious walk, rifles raised at the ready.

Gunny had no intention of being captured or trapped in the room, yet he waited like a cornered hare until the agents were about ten feet from the door. Then with a ferocious roar, he charged from the room firing with the pistol in each hand. One agent managed to squeeze off a shot that missed high and sent plaster down on Gunny's head – but Gunny's aim was true: both agents lay dead or dying in the hallway.

Gunny shoved the two pistols into his waistband and grabbed both rifles from the downed agents. He slung one over his back and readied the other in front of him as he advanced quickly down the hallway. It wouldn't be long before more agents swarmed the building – but for now he had the advantage of surprise and a narrow hallway, preventing him from being engaged from multiple sides.

At the end of the hallway, Gunny exited through the door into the large room with the desk in the middle. Inside, seated at the desk waiting for him as if it was just a regular day, was Agent Grant. Gunny entered the room cautiously, rifle trained on the agent.

"I had better hopes for you Sheriff Gunn," Agent Grant began –

"Save it for someone who cares," Gunny interrupted. "And if you move, I'll blast you."

"That would be a big mistake, seeing how I'm your only hope of walking out of here alive." Agent Grant sat as if unbothered by Gunny's threat. "Outside this building is the full force of Hive. You cannot defeat us. Others – I believe your wife was one of them – have tried and failed."

"And wouldn't you like to see your lovely daughter Tiffany one more time?" Agent Grant continued. "I can make that happen."

"Leave my daughter's name out of your mouth," Gunny spat back angrily.

"She is a sweet thing isn't she? I just might make her my personal s –" Agent Grant's sentence was cut short by the deafening report of gunfire from the rifle in Gunny's hand – and more specifically the gaping hole now in Agent Grant's chest. Agent Grant stared at Gunny, mouth and eyes wide open for a split second, and then his head fell back before his corpse slumped out of the chair onto the ground.

"I've been wanting to do that for a long time," Gunny muttered under his breath as he moved quickly across the room toward the stairway exit. Gunny shot a look at his wristwatch. He'd placed the call to the OKC police only ten minutes ago. He wasn't sure what resources they would send or how long it would take, but he had only one choice, hold out and keep fighting until they arrived.

Entering the dim hallway which led to the stairwell and then outside, Gunny climbed the stairs two at a time, slowing only after he had reached the top. The door leading outside the building had been propped open. Gunny peeked through it. Gunfire answered him.

Jerking backwards, a searing pain shot through his side. In the shadowy, red lighting of the stairway, Gunny could see blood on his hand as he touched his left thigh. As best as he could tell, he'd only taken a ricochet shot rather than a direct hit. It likely wasn't too bad, but still hurt like the dickens – and didn't bode well for his chances.

Gunny contemplated returning downstairs and trying to barricade himself in one of the rooms, but he wasn't sure if there was a backway into the underground area, and the last thing he wanted was to be a fish in a barrel. He needed to get outside where he could see – and if possible, get to his truck where his shotgun and more ammo awaited him. Gunny took a second to reload both pistols before trying again.

A wild charge had worked for him with the two agents downstairs, so Gunny figured he'd try it again. He climbed back up the few stairs he'd retreated down earlier, raised his rifle, and without knowing what he was shooting at, began firing through the doorway, spraying in all directions.

It worked. He saw a handful of Hive agents who'd been taking aim at the doorway, hit the ground and scramble away to cover. Gunny's intent at this point wasn't to hit anyone – just to buy him time to get to his truck. He dropped the rifle, pulled his .40 from his waistband with his left hand and began firing blindly behind him as he raced toward the tailgate of his pickup. About five feet from the rear of the truck, Gunny slid like a baseball player diving into base.

Gunny crept around the backside of the truck to the right side. Peeking around the side, his heart sank. The passenger side door was open. Gunny *knew* he'd not left it like that – meaning that very likely his other weapons and the rest of his ammo were now in Hive's possession. All Gunny had was his two pistols, about seventy-five rounds for each of them, and one of the agent's rifles he'd taken earlier, with probably no more than twenty rounds – enough to kill each agent if they had been stationary targets, but not nearly enough to hold out and keep from being overrun.

Gunny saw a phalanx of five Hive agents walking cautiously toward his truck. He didn't really have a shot on them but fired a couple warning rounds. Deciding to use the bed of his truck as a bunker, he lowered the tailgate and climbed inside. Then he crept forward and peered through the back glass of his truck cab.

It proved to be a critical mistake – a shot rang out and both the windshield and the back glass of his truck shattered, sending glass into Gunny's face. Gunny ducked but his face had been lacerated by the flying glass. Blinking back blood, he wiped his face with the handkerchief from his back pocket. Gunny slid over to the left side of the truck, aimed the rifle down the side and squeezed off a few shots. One of his shots surprisingly struck one of the advancing agents in the stomach and he fell screaming to the ground. The other four agents retreated behind their SUV, dragging their comrade with them.

The courtyard was eerily silent for a couple minutes, until the Grand Matron's voice called out to him, "Paul, you can't win. We can wait as long as necessary. And then you'll be shot again, or bleed out – how's your leg? Don't you see, time is on my side. You'll starve, or give into exhaustion eventually. Your only option is to lay down your weapons and surrender."

"Where's my daughter?" Gunny called back. "I want to see Tiffany."

"She's here," answered the Grand Matron. "And you and she will be reunited just as soon as you drop your weapons and surrender."

Gunny didn't respond immediately, thinking over his options. "We had a deal! Leave my daughter alone and I'd be your dutiful sheriff. You screwed this all up when you took my daughter."

"No, she sealed her fate when she decided to help that meddling detective. You should've controlled your daughter better," the Grand Matron accused.

"So, what now?" Gunny shouted back. "Do me and my daughter go missing like everyone else around here? I'd rather die than join your mindless horde."

"I give you my word that you'll both be spared Detective Cross's fate of my serum," the Grand Matron called back. "But first you have to stop this fruitless standoff. My patience grows thinner with every one of my agents you shoot." The Grand Matron paused momentarily, as if expecting the Sheriff to throw down his weapons and give up. When he didn't, she continued, "Speaking of my agents, what did you do to Agent Grant?"

"Uh, he's having a heart problem – due to the large hole in his chest," the Sheriff shouted back and chuckled. "He had it coming."

"Perhaps so," came the Grand Matron's cold response. "Give this up, Paul. Don't make me involve your daughter."

Gunny saw the wedge of Hive agents begin to creep forward again – a new agent replacing the one he'd just shot. Gunny fired off a half dozen more rounds. None found their mark this time, but it halted their advance.

"Paul. You can't win," came again the voice of the Grand Matron. "Last chance. Think of your daughter."

Gunny closed his eyes. Thoughts of Tiffany and of his wife flashed in his mind. He pushed them away. What hope did he have? He was alone. Captain Durant had not arrived – and maybe he wouldn't after all; maybe he never even believed Gunny's wild story of a small Oklahoma town taken over by a criminal syndicate.

The group of five agents were almost at the front of his truck. Gunny's thoughts were broken by the Grand Matron's voice again, "Paul. Now or never. Don't be a fool."

Gunny looked in his vest pockets at his limited ammo stash. His leg had stiffened where he'd been shot. Blood trickled down his forehead stinging his eyes. "Alright," he finally said. "I'm coming out. I'm laying down my rifle and my two handguns. They're the only weapons I got – I swear it."

Gunny scooted on his rear end back down the truck bed. His left leg burned with intensifying pain.

He dropped gingerly onto his good foot and laid the rifle on the tailgate. He removed his hunting vest and both handguns and laid them down also.

"Alright, I'm unarmed," Gunny shouted. "I'm coming down the left side of the truck."

As he advanced, hands on his head, he could see the barrels of dozens more rifles pointed at him. When he got past the end of his truck, he saw the Grand Matron standing just off to his left, her pistol in her hand at her side. He scanned the area but saw no sign of Tiffany or Detective Cross.

The Grand Matron motioned with her pistol in his direction, and the five agents seized him.

"I'm unarmed. I'm unarmed," he repeated as they pushed him roughly to the ground. His wrists were cuffed behind his back and he was then lifted to his feet and dragged toward the Grand Matron, half-hobbling, half-hopping as he went.

They came to a stop a couple feet in front of the Grand Matron. His towering frame looked down upon the seething woman. "I wanna see my daughter," Gunny demanded.

The Grand Matron gave a slight nod, and on cue, the line of Hive soldiers parted, and an agent pulled Tiffany in Gunny's direction.

"Dad!" Tiffany shouted.

"Hey baby girl," he said with a big grin. "How're we doing?"

As Tiffany drew closer, Gunny could see that she fared little better than he did. Her hair was askew, her face was bloodied and dirty, and the Hive uniform that hung oddly about her slight frame was filthy and ripped.

About fifteen feet from Gunny, Tiffany suddenly kicked the shins of the agent escorting her, ripped her shoulder free from his grasp, and rushed toward her father. The agent charged after her, but Tiffany reached Gunny before he could catch her. She threw her arms around him and sobbed into his chest.

"Shh, it's okay," he softly soothed before Tiffany was snatched away from him by the agent she'd kicked.

"A touching reunion," jeered the Grand Matron. "And I fear a short-lived one.

"Paul, not only have you shot several of my agents," continued the Grand Matron, "but this was all your fault from the beginning. It's your fault that that Detective got here in the first place. You failed to be where you were assigned. You failed to keep him compliant. You failed to control your daughter. A failure is what you are. A failure as a husband. A failure as a father. A failure as a sheriff. And I have no patience or place for failures."

Gunny did not respond but only stared steely down at the much shorter Grand Matron. Suddenly a look of uncontrolled rage crossed her face. She raised her pistol in a swift motion to just underneath Gunny's chin and fired off a single blast.

Tiffany screamed as her father dropped stiffly, dead before he hit the ground.

"Away with her," waved the Grand Matron. "I have no patience for her useless tears. Take her down to the hold. I'll deal with her shortly."

Blood pooled around Sheriff Gunn as Tiffany was dragged away sobbing and screaming. Detective Cross sat motionless and emotionless in an ATV, unaware of the carnage or sorrow nearby – his mind lost in the serum’s grip.

CHAPTER EIGHTEEN

COLLAPSE

Trooper Ferris had been the first to arrive in Hamlin. The town seemed deserted. He drove only a few blocks past the city limits sign and then decided to wait for backup to arrive before venturing any further. Since then, over the last few minutes, nearly twenty other troopers had arrived and formed up on his position.

"What's the story here?" asked one of the other responding troopers. "I just got the call from the Assistant Director himself to get here as fast as I could and await further instructions."

"I spoke briefly to a Captain Durant out of Oklahoma City," answered Trooper Ferris. "He had quite the story to tell." The other troopers moved in closer to hear.

"I guess the sheriff of this town called from some kind of bunker or something underground and said that their town was being held hostage by a gang or mafia – and that it'd been like that for fifty years or more."

"Do what?" said another of the troopers in disbelief, looking up from his phone.

"I'm just telling you what I was told," said Trooper Ferris with a shrug. "He said to be prepared for a fight. Durant's got ATF and OSBI, and a hostage rescue team plus a bunch of ambulances on the way."

"Geez," replied the trooper. "I guess I'd better call my girlfriend and tell her to cancel our dinner plans."

"Good luck with that," said Trooper Ferris. "Something strange is definitely going on here. Neither my radio nor my cell phone work. I had a signal back up the highway, but I lost it a few blocks after I passed the Hamlin signpost. That along with this town being too quiet for my liking – I think there's something to that sheriff's story."

"You ever been here before?" Ferris asked the other trooper.

"Nope, this is a ways out of my patrol area." he said.

"I have," spoke Trooper Russel. All eyes turned on him. "I just remembered. It was a good five or six years ago. Just came in and ate a burger at some burger joint. Other than nobody being terribly friendly, nothing weird stood out. I was in and out of town in probably thirty-five minutes. Never saw anybody but the lady at the restaurant. If she hadn't been there, I'd have sworn this was a ghost town."

"Did your radio work back then?" Ferris asked.

"Couldn't say. I don't think I tried to use it," answered Trooper Russel trying to remember. "Nah, can't remember. Again, I was in and out of here in under an hour."

"Do we have a rally point or target area that we're supposed to be responding to?" asked a trooper that had just driven up. "And what's the story here?"

Ferris was just about to retell the short version when a single gunshot rang out. It sounded like it was a few blocks, maybe half a mile, away.

"I think that's your answer," said Trooper Russel.

"Yeah, uh," mumbled Trooper Ferris looking back through the chicken-scratch notes he'd taken while driving this way. "Captain Durant said the city dump. But he said it was just a front for their base. I looked it up on my phone's map before entering town and losing my signal. Should be just down the road here about a half a mile."

"Do we go ahead and check out that gunshot or wait?" asked Russel.

"It'll only take me five minutes to drive back up the road and get out of this dead zone and get a signal again," answered Ferris. "So let me do that and see first. While I do that, y'all go ahead and gear up – vests, shield if you have them, the works. I'll be back in a jiffy."

Moments later, Trooper Ferris' vehicle squealed a U-turn and sped off. He watched the bars on his cell phone for the signal to return. As soon as it did, he jammed the breaks, pulled to the shoulder, and hit the redial button to call back Captain Durant.

"Durant," said the Captain's strained voice on the other end.

"Hey just looking for your ETA and some orders. Just about five minutes ago we heard a gunshot. Sounded like it came from that dump you were talking about."

Captain Durant cursed. "We're still about forty-five minutes out maybe. I tried radioing you earlier."

"Yeah," answered Trooper Ferris. "Once you drive into town, radios and phones quit working. It's suspicious for sure."

Captain Durant cursed again. "Seems like more and more of that Sheriff Gunn's story checks out. Boy I hate the thought of what we're walking into."

"So you want me to wait or go? We have about twenty of us Troopers here." Ferris replied.

Once again, Captain Durant let out an expletive. "That's up to y'all. I've got the cavalry with me, but like I said we're about forty minutes out."

"You said you got a detective potentially hostage in there?" Ferris asked.

"Yeah Detective Cross – and sounds like the town's sheriff too," answered Captain Durant.

"Gotcha," said Ferris. "That's all I needed to know. Brothers in blue in trouble. We're going in."

"Bless y'all and be safe," came by the answer. "We'll be there just as quick as we can. If it hits the fan, just hunker down and wait."

"Wilco," said Ferris and hung up. Another trooper came flying down the road in his direction, slowing to pull alongside him.

"What's the story?" the trooper asked.

"Follow me into town to where the rest of the guys are and I'll fill you in," answered Ferris, whipping a U-turn, and speeding back into Hamlin.

***

Tiffany was shoved and dragged literally kicking and screaming down the stairs inside the building next to her dad's truck. Moments later, she was pushed into a room and then into a jail cell that was little more than a closet. The door slammed shut behind her and she was plunged into total darkness.

Tiffany kicked the door and then threw her slight frame against it, but it didn't budge. She yelled incoherent sentences and screeched in rage, but to no avail. No one replied. Finally, after several minutes of this, she collapsed to the floor, exhausted.

The cell was so small she couldn't even extend her legs fully in front of her, so she bent her knees and hugged them tightly to her chest.

She tried closing her eyes, but when she did, all she saw were images of her dad dead, of Sam being stabbed with the needle, and of Laura's expressionless face. She wanted to cry, but there were no more tears. It was all too much.

It's over, she thought grimly. *With Dad dead, and Mom – who knows what...*

The thought was too painful to continue.

It was hot and she no longer needed the Hive jacket to blend in, plus she felt disgusting wearing it now, so she took it off. She had taken off her leggings to put on the Hive agent's pants earlier, but now she wished she had kept her leggings. She wanted to be free of her disguise altogether.

In the dark cell, she lost all sense of time. She could've been there twenty minutes or twenty hours. She had no way of knowing.

She remembered what Sam had said earlier that evening about staying in a mild state of dehydration to keep from needing the restroom. She was thankful now that she had listened. She kicked the door a few more times but no one responded.

***

By now there were twenty-three troopers assembled together. They'd geared up and hashed out a quick game plan, so off they drove toward the dump – lights out, sirens off.

They passed no one on the way. About two minutes later, they pulled up outside the dump. Its rusted sheet metal gate was rather unassuming.

Trooper Ferris exited his vehicle, unhooked the strap on his holster and walked cautiously toward the gate. The gate sealed quite tightly, making it impossible to see anything inside. A keypad hung on the wall next to the gate with an intercom button. He pressed the button and waited for a response. None came.

He pressed it again and spoke, "State Police. Open up."

There was a long pause and then a male voice answered, "Unless you have a signed warrant from a judge, you may exit the premises and the town of Hamlin the way you came. Good day."

Ferris quickly pushed the intercom again, "Hey don't you 'good day' me. I heard gunshots coming from in there so I don't need a warrant. Open the gate."

There was no further reply. Trooper Ferris pushed the button again, "This is the Oklahoma State Police. Open the gate or we will force entry."

Ferris pushed on the gate, but it did not budge. It was solid but didn't seem terribly reinforced. Looking over his shoulder to be sure that nobody got the drop on him, he jogged back over to one of the troopers who was driving an SUV.

"Someone inside answered but refused to open. Gate doesn't seem that tough. Probably just chain link with that sheet metal over it. What do you think about ramming it?" asked Ferris.

"Sure, I'll give it a go," responded the trooper.

Ferris quickly organized the other vehicles in a perimeter and the trooper with the SUV prepared to ram the gate. He revved his engine and slammed his bumper into the gate. It shuddered, buckling slightly in the middle, but held firm.

"Again!" shouted Ferris.

The SUV backed up a few feet and then rammed the gate again. This time it popped out of its track and a gap about a foot wide opened. "Almost got it!" shouted the trooper as he backed up for one more run at it. The SUV engine revved and lurched forward again. This time the gate bounced and skidded backwards, tearing from its mounted position and finally falling flat.

A hail of bullets answered the trooper's intrusion. He quickly ducked down and then scrambled into the backseat flinching at the deafening pounding of bullets against the exterior. Glass shattered and rained about him. He managed to get the back hatch open, rolled to the ground, and scampered to safety behind another trooper's car.

"Are you okay?!" Trooper Ferris shouted through the thunder of gunfire from his covered position behind his car.

Ferris couldn't hear a reply, but hoped it was so. Suddenly the front end of the SUV that had breached the gate exploded and flames roared several feet into the air.

"That was no engine fire!" shouted Trooper Ferris. "That was some kind of grenade or something!"

Ferris watched as the SUV smoldered for a moment and then exploded a second time as the gas tank ignited, sending another wave of heat toward the troopers.

So far none of the troopers had fired their weapons. The base sat at the top of an elevated drive – meaning that the troopers hadn't actually seen any hostiles. Ferris mulled what to do. As much as he wanted to storm the compound and locate the missing detective and sheriff, moving forward seemed like a very *bad* idea. They hadn't really known what to expect, but grenades were definitely not on the list.

The gunfire ceased. The only sound was the crackling of flames from the SUV. Trooper Russel crept over to Ferris. "I was a Scout Sniper in the Marines before joining the State Police. I can get up there and check out the situation if you want." Ferris nodded and told him to go ahead.

About five minutes later, Russel's head peeked up over the driveway's crest. Over fifty heavily armed men dressed all in black, carried military-grade rifles, some with grenade launchers – all pointed toward the compound's entrance. They also had a dozen or so black SUVs and jeeps arranged for cover. The compound appeared to have three buildings – one that looked like an office, one that looked like a hangar perhaps, and one that looked like a dorm or barracks.

Trooper Russel scooted back down the steep driveway and reported back to Ferris. "Yeah," Ferris conceded, "We're just gonna have to wait for Durant to get here with the feds. No way we can go up against those numbers and that firepower without more of us."

"How long did the Captain say it'd be before he got here?" Russel asked

"He said about forty minutes – and that was a while ago. Should be soon. Why don't you drive back up the road and get a signal and check in," Ferris suggested. "Here's my phone, just call back the last number. Passcode is 1611."

***

Russel nodded, hopped in his car, and sped away. As soon as he saw bars on the phone reappear, he whipped to the highway shoulder and hit the redial button.

"Hey Ferris, Durant here," came back the voice on the other end. "I'm almost there. In fact, I think I can see you. Is that you on the side of the road?"

"Yep, but actually this is Trooper Russel. Ferris is at the city dump holding things down. We had quite the welcome from those perps."

"Hey not to cut you off, but let's get back down there and you and Ferris can fill me in. I've got a man to save," replied Captain Durant curtly.

"Roger that," answered Russel and hung up. He whipped his car around back on the road and sped back into the strange little town called Hamlin.

***

Tiffany must've somehow managed to fall asleep, but she was awakened by the door opening and a beam of light blinding her. It was the Grand Matron.

"Get up. Come with me," she ordered.

It was dark except for the light from the Grand Matron's flashlight. The Grand Matron cuffed Tiffany behind her back and then prodded her forward roughly.

"Where are you taking me?" Tiffany demanded.

"Shut up and move," was all the Grand Matron said.

They exited the cell block into a hallway. A minute later they were ascending the stairs leading outside. Tiffany blinked as they stepped into the Oklahoma sunlight. Her dad's truck was still there but she looked away when she saw his body in the truck bed. Instead of going toward the front of the compound, the Grand Matron ushered her toward the false wall and Greytown.

Tiffany yelled for help, not knowing who might hear. "Where are we going?" Tiffany asked again.

"For a little ride," was the Grand Matron's cryptic reply.

They passed through the holographic wall and immediately Tiffany heard the whine of a helicopter's motor. The Grand Matron took off running, dragging Tiffany awkwardly along.

***

It didn't take long for Captain Durant and the feds to coordinate a strike plan with Ferris' troopers. The hostage rescue team's armored van took point along with the OSBI's counter terrorism team. Using a megaphone mounted on the armored van, Captain Durant demanded a complete disarmament inside the compound.

"We have scores of officers ready to storm the compound with deadly force. Place your weapons down. Do not resist or we will shoot!"

With Madam Von Druska on the run and Agent Grant dead, the leaderless Hive surrendered without another shot being fired. Officers and feds flooded the compound and soon everyone in the courtyard was cuffed and face down in the dirt.

"Who's in charge here?" demanded Captain Durant. His question was met with silence.

Agent 32 finally spoke up, "It's the Grand Matron you'll want to be talking to. None of us here are in charge of anything. We just follow orders."

"Alright, so where's this Grand Matron?"

"Who knows? Gone probably via the airfield."

"Which direction is the airfield?"

"Behind the buildings."

Captain Durant looked and saw only a back wall. "Quit wasting time! There's nothing back there."

"Things are not always what they seem with Hive," Agent 32 replied coyly.

Captain Durant pressed, but the agent wouldn't divulge more.

Durant asked changing subjects. "Where's Sheriff Gunn?"

"Dead," was the agent's flat reply. "The Grand Matron offed him for starting this whole mess."

"That might've been the gunshot we heard a while back," said Trooper Ferris sadly.

Dread filled Captain Durant. "And what of Detective Cross?"

"Not dead," answered the agent with a laugh. Captain Durant peppered the agent for more information, but to no avail.

Captain Durant and the hostage rescue team ran to the back of the compound in the direction the agent had indicated was the airfield. One of the team-members pointed out a pair of deep ruts in the dirt indicating a fight or struggle taking place. They led right into the back wall.

Captain Durant scratched his head. It seemed as if the trail went right *through* the wall. *Maybe there's some kind of hidden gate or door*, he thought. He went to lean with his hand on the wall to feel for a hidden doorway and almost fell as his hand passed through the wall. He jerked his hand back as if expecting something to bite it.

"A hologram," Captain Durant exclaimed. Despite his amazement, he motioned for the hostage rescue team to move forward.

On the other side, Captain Durant was greeted with the whir of helicopter blades. To their left was a helipad and a woman struggled to shove a handcuffed individual inside the helicopter's side door.

Captain Durant and the hostage rescue team ran toward them. Captain Durant shouted, "Halt or we'll be forced to shoot!" but his words were drowned out by the helicopter engine. One of the team members took aim with his rifle and fired three quick shots at the tail rotor of the helicopter. It sputtered, smoked, and then came to a stop.

Still advancing, Captain Durant repeated his orders for them to stop. He could now tell that the woman's captive was another woman – perhaps a teenager. He watched as the woman dropped her hand to her side where a holster held a pistol. "Do not reach for it!" Captain Durant ordered. "My team will shoot. We don't want to, but we will if you reach for your weapon or attempt to harm the girl in any way."

The woman froze as if deciding what to do – her hand hovering inches above the holster at her waist. He motioned for the hostage rescue team-members to aim their weapons at the woman. "If she goes for it, take the shot," he ordered in a low voice.

About twenty agonizing seconds passed, and then Captain Durant saw the woman's shoulders slump signaling defeat. The girl she'd been holding hostage broke free and ran frantically toward them, her hands still cuffed behind her back. When she was about ten feet away, one of the hostage rescue team-members ordered her to the ground, and took her into custody. Captain Durant and the rest of the team advanced cautiously on her captor.

"That's the Grand Matron! Don't let her get away," the young lady called after him.

With the helicopter disabled and nowhere to go, before long the woman also was in custody, along with the Hive agent in the cockpit of the helicopter. Captain Durant demanded her identity, but she gave no reply.

***

Tiffany watched as the Grand Matron was led away. As soon as the officer-in-charge returned, Tiffany began speaking a-mile-a-minute. "My name is Tiffany Gunn. My dad –" Her voice cracked. "My dad was the sheriff – until that horrid woman murdered him in cold blood," she screamed more in the direction of the Grand Matron than to the officer.

The officer reached down and removed Tiffany's handcuffs. "I'm Captain Durant from the Oklahoma City Police Department. You can tell me everything. You're safe now."

"Do you know where Sam is? We've got to find him."

"Wait, Detective Sam Cross? You know him?"

"Yes of course! "We've been working together for the last two days, or is it three? It's been such a blur – but anyway we've been working together to take down Hive and rescue my best friend Laura. We stopped the production of their mind control serum before we both got captured..."

"Whoa, slow down young lady," Captain Durant interrupted. "Mind control serum?"

"I'm trying to explain," Tiffany continued impatiently. "Anyway, after we got captured, the Grand Matron injected Sam, I mean Detective Cross, with the serum and so now he's basically a zombie. But it wears off in about two days – or so we think. I hope…" her voice trailed off.

"Wow. Ok. What else?" asked Captain Durant.

"You see that building up there," Tiffany continued, pointing at what looked like a large factory. "That's where they made the serum. And there's a bunch, probably a couple hundred, people from Hamlin in there who've been kidnapped and given the serum and so they're mind-controlled as well."

"And that other building," she said pointing at what kind of looked like a small stadium. "There's a whole bunch more of their mind-controlled people in there too, including my best friend. In Hamlin we call them the Missing. I don't think there should be that many Hive agents left in there. We took out like four."

"Okay," said Captain Durant slowly, as if trying to take in everything Tiffany had just told him. "Do you have any idea where Detective Cross might be?"

"Last I saw him, he was back in the main compound," answered Tiffany. "You might've not noticed him and thought he was a Hive agent. As you can see," she said, pointing at her pants, "we were trying to blend in and be undercover. Sam, I mean Detective Cross, was in black pants and a black shirt and may have had a ski mask on."

"Ok that's enough for now," Captain Durant said. "Let's go."

The Grand Matron was already out of sight and Tiffany and Captain Durant walked back to the compound. Back in the compound, the other officers had begun lining up the Hive agents for transport. Captain Durant informed Trooper Ferris of what Tiffany had said about several hundred mind-controlled townsfolk on the other side of the false wall. Ferris let out a long low whistle at the mention of a mind-controlling drug. He and about thirty other troopers and officers mounted the Hive's SUVs and drove to check it out.

Meanwhile, Tiffany began looking for Sam. After a couple minutes she let out an exuberant yell. "Captain! He's right here!"

Captain Durant ran over. Sam's face was smudged black and crusted in blood. "Cross, can you hear me?" he shouted, but Sam just stared blankly ahead.

"I told you, the Grand Matron injected him with the serum," Tiffany said.

"Get one of the EMT's and a stretcher over here!" shouted Captain Durant.

One of the officers ran up to Captain Durant and reported, "I think I found the equipment that was jamming our comms. It should be off now so we can make calls out."

"That's great. Call in for more officers and more feds," the Captain replied. "And you better get additional ambulances and some transport busses down here. CSI as well. Oh," he added in a low voice as he glanced at Tiffany, "A coroner as well. They killed the town's sheriff."

"Yeah, sad deal," the officer replied grimly. "I think I saw him over by that pickup. Looks like they just tossed him in the bed."

"C'mon miss," Captain Durant said to Tiffany. "You should get checked by the EMT's."

"I'm fine," replied Tiffany. "I know I don't look it – but really, I am."

"All the same," Captain Durant urged.

Within a couple hours, hundreds of vehicles had descended upon the small town of Hamlin. The whole compound and half the town was crawling with every kind of law enforcement agency imaginable. Hamlin would never be the same – but that was actually a good thing.

***

Back in Oklahoma City, Detective Cross's wife and boys sat in a hospital room. Sam lay in the bed in a medically induced coma while the doctors flushed the serum out of his system. A couple rooms down, Tiffany also sat in one of those uncomfortable chairs that hospital rooms always have, watching her best friend sleep. Before going to the hospital, Tiffany had convinced one of the police officers to take her by her house so she could change. She'd chosen a sleeveless shirt and shorts – but now she wished she'd opted for something warmer. The hospital was freezing. She pulled a thin blanket that a nurse had given more tightly around her shoulders.

The concentration of the serum's dose in Laura's system had been much lower than what was in Sam and so the doctors decided to let the drugs pass from her naturally. It was weird for Tiffany to watch her friend, sometimes asleep, sometimes awake, but her mind not there. With Laura on the drugs for only two weeks, the doctors said they didn't think there would be any lasting damage or strong withdrawals. The other Missing wouldn't be so lucky. The doctors were only guessing – having never dealt with the serum before. But they implied that some of the Missing might require long-term mental health care.

Tiffany's thoughts were interrupted by Laura sitting up in the bed and rubbing her eyes. "Tiff, is that you?" spoke Laura coherently for the first time. "What on earth...where am I?"

Tiffany jumped up and ran to her and gave her a big hug. "Laura!" she squealed. "Maybe I should tell you after you're a little more awake and had some real food – if you can call this hospital food 'food.' But the last week has been *cuh-razy*!"

Tiffany sat on the edge of the bed, and about thirty minutes later, while Laura ate bites of a sandwich from the hospital cafeteria, Tiffany slowly recounted the last few days.

The next day Detective Cross woke up. His wife, Jennifer, and their two boys peppering him with kisses while Captain Durant filled him in on what had happened since he'd been drugged. The Grand Matron and the rest of Hive had been booked and were scheduled to face a federal judge later that week. Sam had been put in for the Medal of Valor and a promotion for his bravery – along with two weeks paid leave, which the Cross boys did their best to convince their dad that it meant a trip to Disney was in order. Tiffany and Laura popped in and Laura thanked Sam for all he'd done.

Later that week one of the largest state-wide funerals ever was held for Sheriff Paul Gunn. He was hailed as a hero and loving father, having gone after his daughter and given his life to save her and their little town. Both state Senators attended the funeral and there were talks of the Presidential Medal being awarded him posthumously. Counselors began working with Hamlin's folks to undo the effects of living as prisoners their whole lives and to help them return to normalcy in the outside world.

***

After the funeral Sam caught up with Tiffany. "So what are your plans? Back to Hamlin to run that restaurant you talked about?"

"Nah. I'm done with Hamlin," Tiffany replied with a slightly disgusted tone. "There's nothing for me left there. Mom wasn't one of the Missing – or if she was, she died long ago. I heard they found a mass grave in Greytown, but it'll take them a while to identify those buried there. I've been talking to Laura. She still wants to go to the State College in OKC and I've decided to join her."

"That's great. Any clue what you'll study?" Sam asked.

"I haven't one hundred percent decided yet. I'm a seasoned crime fighter now though," she said with a wink. "Maybe Criminal Justice. Maybe Crime Scene Forensics. I'm not sure. I don't think I have to decide day one."

"That'd be great," replied Sam. Tiffany definitely had the smarts for Criminal Justice and the guts.

"Hey," continued Sam, changing the subject, "I don't want to make things weird, but since you're gonna be in the city – don't be a stranger. Let me keep an eye on you. It's a wild world out here."

"Out here?" said Tiffany with a laugh. "I have a feeling OKC will be tame compared to where I've lived all my life."

"Okay. Let me know if you change your mind," Sam replied.

"No, that's not what I mean," laughed Tiffany again. "I'd love to stay in touch. Your wife seems lovely and your boys are the cutest ever."

"Awesome. You're welcome over anytime – Laura too," Sam said. "And I'm serious. If you *ever* need anything at all, if anyone gives you any trouble – anything, just holler."

Tiffany gave Sam a hug, wiped away a tear, and headed back to rejoin Laura.

***

In the coming weeks, several Hive agents broke their silence to gain lesser sentences and revealed the global schemes of their organization. Not long after, in an open-and-shut trial, the Grand Matron Von Druska was sentenced to life in a Colorado supermax federal prison without the possibility of parole.

Sam returned to fight crime – though Captain Durant often joked with him that he wasn't allowed to have any more stolen car cases. Tiffany and Laura went to the state college. And Hamlin remained a small town with no traffic light and the perfect place to get a burger – with a crazy story on the side.

The End

ABOUT THE AUTHOR

Stephen Zimmerman was born in a small town in west Texas. From Texas, to Oklahoma, Missouri and Africa, simplicity and modest living shaped Stephen's childhood. In 2006, Stephen joined the United States Air Force. During this time, he served two tours in the Middle East and was awarded a Commendation Medal, seven Air Medals, and the rank of Staff Sergeant. That same year Stephen also met his wife Leanna, and they were married in Spring 2007. Together they have four children, two dogs, and six fish tanks. In 2012, Stephen graduated with a Bachelor of Arts in Biblical Studies and began his pastoring career in Arizona in 2015.

When not with work or family, Stephen enjoys devouring True Crime, psychology, and anything mysterious. This passion has blended those elements into a love for writing stories of his own.

www.GlobalPublishGroup.com

Made in the USA
Middletown, DE
11 October 2021

49904350R00136